MW01088195

JUST A LITTLE CRUSH

NEW YORK TIMES BESTSELLING AUTHORS

Carly Phillips

Erika Wilde

CHAPTER ONE

Stevie

"COME ON, VAL," I called out to my sister, who was still in the bathroom getting ready, or maybe even stalling. "I don't want to be late, considering this *is* a surprise birthday party for Raven." I'd met Raven, who was one of my closest friends in the city, through my waitressing job at The Back Door in Manhattan.

A few minutes later, Valerie finally emerged. While she looked beautiful in a modest black dress, and her makeup and blonde bobbed hair were on point for the occasion, her face showed the emotional toll the past weeks had taken. The depression she'd fallen into after leaving her abusive ex wasn't hard for me to miss, and I hated that my sister's normal vibrant personality had been dimmed by Mark Branson, aka the entitled asshole.

My sister was all I had in the world and I wasn't about to lose her the same way we'd lost our mother when our father had choked her to death during one of his drunken rages. Which was why, when Mark had been out golfing the Saturday after I'd seen a bruise on Val's cheek, I'd packed up her things and had moved her into my place.

It didn't matter that I lived in a very miniscule one-bedroom apartment in Elmhurst, Queens, which was all I could afford on my earnings as a waitress and intern at Dare PR two days a week. There was no denying it was cramped having Valerie live here with me, but I didn't care. The only thing that mattered to me was knowing she was safe and out of Mark's clutches.

Not that Mark hadn't continued harassing Valerie after the breakup. He'd basically stalked her, physically and through texts, and even though I'd convinced Valerie to get a restraining order against him, the whole situation had caused my sister to become more withdrawn and she'd isolated herself in my apartment.

Which was the main reason why I'd insisted Valerie accompany me to tonight's party. To give her some normalcy and get her out in public again so she didn't become a complete shut-in. I wanted to see that spark back in her eyes, along with the confidence she'd had before Mark had systematically broken her down.

"You look amazing," I told her, trying to boost her morale. "And you're going to have a great time tonight. Knowing Remy, he went all out with the food, and the entertainment will be top-notch. The guy doesn't do things halfway, not when it comes to Raven."

Valerie didn't look convinced about joining me.

"I'm sure you'd have a much better time at the party without me tagging along."

"Not true," I argued with a smile as I slipped into a pair of heels. "I need a dance partner, and you'll do just fine."

She scoffed. "I'm so not in the mood to dance and party."

"Too bad. I've already told Remy that you're my plus-one," I said, not allowing her any excuses to try and get out of tonight's festivities. "And I want to introduce you to Samantha Dare, my boss at Dare PR, who you haven't met yet." With any luck, I'd be able to help Valerie land herself a job at the marketing firm I worked at.

"Why would she be there?" Valerie asked curiously.

"She's engaged to Remy's brother, Dex." With over fifty invited guests, I was certain the entire Sterling family was going to be there, along with close friends and coworkers from the bar.

"I hate that you're going to be essentially babysitting me," she said, then a glimmer of a smile touched her lips. "What you *should* be doing is putting the moves on Caleb," she said of Raven's brother, who Valerie had met in passing at The Back Door. "You look gorgeous in that sexy little pink dress."

"What, this old thing?" I spun around playfully, causing the ruffled skirt to flare out around my knees. But truthfully, the dress really was a few years old and bought at a secondhand store, where I did most of my

CARLY PHILLIPS & ERIKA WILDE

shopping to save money.

"You make old look very new and chic," Valerie complimented, then tipped her head inquisitively. "I'm assuming Caleb is going to be there tonight?"

I shrugged as if I didn't care one way or another, which was a lie. The thought of seeing Caleb outside of him stopping into the bar to see Raven, or being at a get-together because of our mutual connection to Raven, did make butterflies flutter in my stomach. "Probably, since I doubt he'd miss his sister's surprise birthday party."

"Well, he's going to take one look at you and his jaw is going to drop." That familiar humor of Valerie's was apparent in her tone. "He might even drool."

I grinned at the image she'd created as I pulled up my rideshare app and summoned a car for the drive into the city. Since I didn't live in the greatest neighborhood, and I still didn't trust that Mark wasn't lurking about, Valerie and I would wait until the car arrived before heading downstairs to the curb.

"Yeah, well, I'm not going to the party to see Caleb," I said, glancing back at Valerie with a smile. "It's all about Raven tonight, and you and I having a good time together."

"It could be all about you and Caleb having a good time together, and he would be far better company than me." Valerie picked up her own purse. "I've been in the bar and I've seen the way he looks at you when you're working. Like he's hungry...and not for the food."

I shivered, because I'd seen that look, too—not that Caleb had ever acted on the attraction between us. Then again, according to Raven he'd been through the wringer with his ex-wife who was still trying to gain full custody of their six-year-old son, Owen, and hooking up with me was undoubtedly the lowest priority on his list.

"The man is way out of my league," I said, which was the truth considering how obscenely wealthy Caleb was—from family money, and his rise as a real estate mogul—and that our social circle beyond Raven did not overlap. "Yes, there's an attraction, and we've flirted, but we've known each other for over a year and it's not like he's taken the initiative to ask me out or anything."

Valerie tipped her head thoughtfully, causing her bobbed hair to slide across her jawline. "Maybe he just needs a little incentive, and you being a little more forward. When was the last time you got laid?"

"Way too long," I admitted with a sigh. I'd casually dated since moving to New York a few years ago, but I was selective about who I slept with and no one had appealed to me on a physical and sexual level, which meant my vibrator got quite the workout. "Besides, Caleb is my best friend's brother, and as much as I'd love for him to end my dry spell, that's not going to happen."

"Too bad," Valerie said as a mischievous look shimmered in her eyes. "It's hard not to notice that he's got that whole big dick energy thing going on. All that quiet confidence, those power suits he wears, and that dominant, alpha edge."

I laughed, though I was enjoying this playful conversation with my sister, after weeks of her more morose, depressed demeanor. It felt like she was turning a corner back to her old self and I was grateful.

"Big dick energy," I mused, then giggled. "Hmm. I'd love to know if that BDE extends to what's beneath those power suits."

"There's only one way to find out," Valerie said meaningfully, just as my phone pinged, announcing our ride was at the curb.

"Stop being such an instigator." I narrowed my eyes at her, but I was smiling.

"Who, me?" Valerie batted her lashes my way.

"Yes, *you*." I grabbed the wrapped gift for Raven off the small dining table, then hooked my arm through Valerie's as we headed toward the door. "Behave yourself tonight."

"I make no promises," she said.

I was secretly glad to see this feisty side to Valerie reemerging, and by the time we arrived at our destination—Hotel Hendricks in Midtown—it was clear that her mood had lifted exponentially, as if getting out of the apartment was just what my sister needed. We made our way up to the twenty-ninth floor to Daintree, a rooftop lounge that had been reserved for Raven's private party for the night.

It was a beautiful September evening, just cool and breezy enough to be comfortable, though the well-placed heat lamps helped keep any chill at bay. Outdoor mood lighting set the tone for casual elegance, and the spacious terrace had been transformed to accommodate over fifty people, with an area for dinner, various sitting areas with firepits, and even a dance floor with a DJ who was currently playing background music.

Guests milled about, enjoying the full-service bar and the trays of hors d'oeuvres being offered by the waitstaff. Since there was still about twenty minutes before Remy arrived with Raven, Valerie and I selected one of the fruity cocktails making the rounds, crafted specifically for Raven's party.

"Here's to a fun evening," I said, and clinked my glass to Valerie's.

We both took a sip of the delicious concoction, my gaze scanning the area for a familiar face…and found one when my eyes connected with Caleb's across the way. He looked breathtakingly gorgeous in a dark gray suit and all that BDE on display.

Instantaneous flutters rose in my stomach, and I would have been okay with that reaction if my damn nipples hadn't followed suit, tightening in pure sexual awareness against the silky fabric of my dress. And between my thighs? Well, that tingling sensation made me shift restlessly in my heels in an effort to chase away the ache settling there.

He was standing with Dex Sterling and Max Corbin, the other two men conversing while a sexy smile curved Caleb's lips as he subtly raised his own drink at me and inclined his head in a silent greeting. There was no missing the slow, appreciative perusal of his gaze as it traversed the length of my figure, wreaking havoc once again with my body and making me feel all sorts of ways.

Dex said something, diverting Caleb's attention, much to my relief.

"See." Valerie elbowed me gently in the side so I didn't spill my drink. "He's already eating you up."

There was no denying what had been so apparent, even if I knew it would lead to nothing between Caleb and me. "Stop," I said, giving my sister a mock-stern look.

She took another sip of her drink, clearly enjoying herself at my expense. "Maybe he's too shy to make the first move."

I almost choked on the drink I was taking of my cocktail, because a man like Caleb, with such a commanding presence, was the opposite of shy. "Maybe he's just fine with us being friends," I said, because we were at least that.

I'd known Caleb over a year now, and there had been many gatherings because of our connection to Raven that put us in close proximity. We'd had plenty of casual, *friendly* conversations, some even a bit flirty, so I wasn't about to read anything more into our interactions.

Valerie shrugged, looking unconvinced. "Okay, if you say so."

"I do, so behave," I reminded her beneath my

breath, just as I caught sight of Samantha Dare, my direct boss where I was interning at Dare PR while finishing up my marketing degree online. I hoped to stay on with the firm once I earned my degree in the next few months. That would mean a nice salary to compensate what I made at the bar, and it would enable me to move to a nicer apartment and better neighborhood.

"There's my boss, who I want you to meet." I grabbed Valerie's elbow and guided her in that direction, discarding our empty cocktail glasses on the way.

Samantha was chatting with her best friend, Brandy, who was also her office manager at the PR firm. They both smiled at me as we approached.

"Hi, Samantha, Brandy," I acknowledged each of them. "I'd like you to meet my sister, Valerie."

"It's a pleasure," Samantha said amicably, shaking Valerie's hand.

"Likewise," my sister said, before exchanging the same greeting with Brandy.

We made small talk for a while and when the time was right, I returned my attention back to Brandy. "I know this isn't the best place to do this but I know you're looking for a new assistant, and Valerie is experienced and looking for a new job."

Brandy's eyebrows raised, perked up in interest.

"I just wanted the two of you to meet face to face before she sent in her résumé." I didn't explain that Valerie was currently unemployed, or that her ex, a junior advisor and the son of the CEO at the financial firm where she'd worked as a secretary, had gotten her fired in retribution for her not going back to him. That was my sister's story to tell, if she chose to.

"Wonderful. It's always so much easier when someone comes recommended," Brandy said, genuinely enthusiastic as she withdrew a business card from her purse and handed it to Valerie. "Send your résumé directly to me at that email address, and we'll go from there."

"Thank you," Valerie said, her eyes wide with surprise. "I appreciate that."

"Of course. We love having Stevie in the office. If you're as hardworking as she is, then we'd be lucky to have you on board."

Samantha glanced at something, or someone, over my shoulder and smirked as she nudged Brandy. "I think our men are getting restless." She looked back at me. "They're waving us over, so excuse us for now."

"Of course." I looked in the direction where Dex and Max had been conversing with Caleb, but he was no longer with them.

"Wow. Brandy didn't have to do that," Valerie said, staring at the business card in awe. "I would have gone through the regular channels of applying for the job."

"Well, now you don't have to. At least not completely. You'll still have to get through an interview and prove yourself."

She bit her bottom lip, and I could see her insecurities surfacing. "And what about explaining getting fired from my previous job?"

I touched Valerie's arm reassuringly. "Technically, you weren't fired. You were let go. And trust me when I say that these women are very understanding." I lowered my voice so only Valerie could hear me. "Samantha had a crazy ex, so both she and Brandy are going to be more sympathetic to your situation than you realize. So be honest and tell them what happened with Mark and his petty revenge."

She nodded and exhaled a deep breath. "You're right. And this is very exciting. I mean, Dare PR is one of the most highly respected firms in the city."

I loved seeing that enthusiasm in Valerie's eyes. That sense of purpose that had been missing for weeks now. "Yes, I know. And how fun would it be to work together at the same place?"

Valerie tucked the card into her purse and grinned. "Very."

A member of the waitstaff walked up to us, a silver tray in hand that he extended our way. "Would either of you care for an oyster on the half shell with a simple mignonette?" he offered.

I tried not to gag at the gross-looking mollusk. I knew that this particular hors d'oeuvre was a high-end delicacy, of course, and Remy had spared no expense for this lavish affair for his wife, but I wasn't about to indulge.

"No, thank you," I said as politely as I could manage.

Valerie shrugged. "Sure, I'll try one."

I watched as my sister brought the shell to her lips, tipped it up, and the grayish blob of meat slid into her mouth. She chewed a couple of times, then swallowed, giving a thoughtful "Hmm" as she returned the now empty shell to a discard dish on the tray.

I shuddered and grimaced through the whole process, and as soon as the waiter walked away, I said, "Oh my God, that looked disgusting."

"It really wasn't that bad."

A low, masculine chuckle sounded from beside me. Startled, I glanced to my left and found Caleb standing there. My pulse ricochetted in shock, and pleasure.

"Sorry," he said, flashing one of those charming grins of his. "I came over to say hello and couldn't help but overhear your amusing conversation."

"There is nothing amusing about a raw oyster," I insisted, trying not to let my little crush on this man show.

He pushed his hands into the front pockets of his slacks, which pulled his suit jacket a little tighter across his solid chest. "You should have tried one. They're an aphrodisiac, you know."

I laughed and shook my head. "Nope. Something that slimy has no business being an aphrodisiac."

"Fair enough." Mirth danced in his stunning blue eyes as they held mine, making my heart race a bit faster. "I suppose chocolate and pomegranates are more to your liking?"

"If seduction is the goal, then yes," I said, the

words leaving my mouth before I could censor them. Not that I really cared when it was the truth.

He arched a dark brow, looking intrigued. "Duly noted."

We stared at one another, as if nothing and no one else existed around us. It was times like this, when the chemistry between us was so palpable, when the flirtations were rife with innuendos, that I wanted to throw caution to the wind and do something wild and reckless. Like press myself against his hard body, or kiss him, just to see if that restraint of his crumbled and BDE took over.

My sister cleared her throat, shattering the moment between us, and Caleb glanced at her, a friendly smile easing across his lips. "Valerie, right?" he asked, acknowledging her when I'd forgotten she even existed.

Valerie smiled back. "Correct. It's nice to see you, Caleb. And I promise, my sister is far more adventurous than her discriminating attitude toward those oysters shows."

I gaped at her, and she gave me a too innocent wide-eyed look, while Caleb's low chuckle roused all my senses and slid down my spine like a warm, masculine caress.

Someone dinged a piece of silverware against a crystal glass, the loud sound cutting through the buzz of conversation out on the terrace. "Everyone, gather around. Remy is on his way up with Raven, so get ready to yell surprise when she walks through those doors."

The guests huddled closer together, and as we did so, we got separated from Caleb, who ended up standing on the other side of the group with his younger sister, Cara. He should have been looking at the entrance to the restaurant for Raven's arrival, but instead his eyes remained on me, that slight, sexy smile wreaking havoc with my entire body.

"That man is going to feed you chocolates and pomegranates the first chance he gets," Valerie teased.

I finally glanced away from Caleb's arousing stare to roll my eyes at my sister. "Trust me. The two of us are all flirt and no action." It wasn't the first time we'd indulged in playful, sexy banter, and it never went further than that—much to my disappointment.

Less than a minute later, Remy escorted Raven out onto the terrace. We all shouted "Surprise," startling the shit out of my best friend, who stared at everyone in shock, then smacked her husband on the chest for pulling off such a stunt. Remy took it all in stride and merely pulled Raven into his arms. She went willingly, thanking him with a kiss and a beaming smile.

I sighed as I watched them with an undeniable amount of envy. I couldn't help it. These two were so perfect together. Remy, normally so unflappable as a boss, was complete mush for his wife, and I couldn't have been happier for Raven who'd been through so much and had finally found her person.

The festivities commenced. The cocktail hour was wrapped up, followed by a delicious three-course dinner by a Michelin chef, then the dance floor opened up as the DJ played upbeat tunes. I coaxed Valerie to join me as my dance partner, along with the women who couldn't convince their husbands or better halves to let loose. After a while I could tell she was starting to get fatigued, probably hitting her limit of socializing for the evening.

Between songs, as we took a break to grab a glass of water, she gave me a tired smile. "I've really had a great time tonight, and I'm glad I came, but I think I'm going to head home."

I understood. Considering how depressed she'd been lately, this was more stimulation than she was used to. "Okay. Just let me say my goodbyes and we'll head out."

She shook her head, her expression adamant. "No, you stay and enjoy yourself. I don't want you leaving because of me, and before you argue," she went on, just as I opened my mouth to do that. "I'm a big girl and I'll be fine. And, I have that pepper spray in my purse," she said, which I'd bought for her after Mark's stalking and threats. "I'll keep it in my hand at all times, and I promise I'll text you when I get home and I'm locked in the apartment."

Despite all her assurances, I still wanted to protest, but I knew that Valerie wasn't going to back down. I also knew that I couldn't smother her and needed to respect her wishes. "Fine." I gave her a hug. "But I'll be checking my phone obsessively until I know you're safe and locked in the apartment."

"Fair enough." She summoned an Uber, and by the time I walked with her back down to the front of the hotel, her ride was there.

After another promise to let me know when she arrived home, she was gone. I headed back up to the terrace, stopping to use the bathroom and touch up my makeup and fluff my wavy blonde hair, while texting back and forth with Valerie during her ride. A half an hour later, when she assured me she was locked in for the night, only then did I allow myself to rejoin the girls out on the dance floor.

I hadn't talked to Caleb since that initial conversation before Raven's arrival to the party, but I was very aware of his presence as the night went on. Currently, he was sitting at a table with his sister Cara, but when the DJ played "Macarena" she couldn't resist joining in on the fun. Us girls laughed as we attempted the specific choreography, and the few times I glanced Caleb's way his eyes were on me as I swayed to the beat, gyrated my hips along with everyone else, and shook my ass when applicable.

I figured if I couldn't have Caleb, I could at least show him what he was missing out on.

CHAPTER TWO

Caleb

I COULDN'T KEEP my eyes off her, which was par for the course when it came to Stevie Palmer, a woman who tempted me more than any other had in a very long time. Probably because she was so different from the overtly sophisticated women I'd once dated.

Like now, I watched as she danced without inhibition, laughing and enjoying the moment with friends. She was like a breath of fresh air, with a bubbly, upbeat personality—even when I'd seen her exhausted at the end of her waitressing shift at The Back Door.

She was fun and lighthearted. There were no airs or pretenses when it came to Stevie. She didn't go out of her way to try and impress me—something I hated when it came to the women in my social circle—which was why I found it so easy to just be myself around her. To flirt with her, even…because we'd been able to do so without either of us expecting anything more.

She was certainly the polar opposite of my ex-wife, Alyssa, who looked down on those she felt were inferior and not a part of the elite, privileged world she'd grown up in. And that snobby, judgmental attitude had only gotten worse over the years since I'd divorced her.

I'd been raised in that same world as Alyssa, with familial expectations I hadn't adhered to. I'd bucked convention after my father died and my mother expected me to take a position in the family's legal consulting firm working with my uncle. Instead, I'd chosen to make my own way and go into real estate as an investor and a broker. Cassandra Kane had been mortified, pissed even that I wasn't upholding the family tradition, but now that I was a partner at Manhattan Prestige Realty and owned a multitude of properties and buildings, and was undoubtedly even richer than my uncle, my mother had finally, begrudgingly, accepted my choice of career.

A mother who wasn't here tonight to celebrate Raven's birthday because Raven had cut Cassandra out of her life when she'd chosen her psychotic son—my fucking twin brother—over her adopted daughter. It was difficult for me to even maintain a civil relationship with my mother, but I did it for Owen, because he deserved to have both sets of grandparents in his life.

Sitting by one of the firepits by myself and sipping my last bourbon of the night, I considered the woman who consumed too much of my thoughts. Maybe if so much of my life wasn't in upheaval, I would have asked Stevie out on a date. But I had an ex-wife just waiting for the chance to skew anything to her advantage during our ongoing custody battle for Owen. And then there was my mother, who commiserated and sided with Alyssa and tried to make me feel guilty for divorcing her. But I had zero regrets about ending our marriage, and no matter how much Alyssa wanted a reconciliation—and was using custody of Owen to persuade me to give her another chance—it wasn't going to happen.

On top of all that emotional turmoil, I was still dealing with the fact that Lance, my shitty deranged twin, was serving a very long sentence in prison for his assault on Raven, violating parole, and racking up federal charges for calling in a bomb threat. Some days it felt like I was just trying to pick up the pieces of my life and keep them glued together.

My sole focus right now was Owen and keeping Alyssa from finding a way to gain full custody. That in itself was a challenge, considering I knew she'd grasp any opportunity to make that happen, just to spite me for divorcing her, even if my reasons for doing so had been legitimate. Dealing with her was exhausting, but all I cared about was making sure my son had some kind of stability in his life and didn't feel torn between two parents, even if Alyssa didn't give a damn about any of that.

Stevie's unfettered laughter drew my attention back to her, the sound calming and distracting me, in a good way. I shoved all those troubling personal thoughts to the back of my mind and watched as she danced with friends and had a good time. Sitting off on my own, I allowed myself to appreciate the bounce of her breasts as she shimmied her shoulders and the provocative way she shook her ass to the beat of the music. Every once in a while she glanced my way and I couldn't help but wonder if she was deliberately teasing and tempting me.

I was most definitely tempted, because those initial thoughts drifted to much dirtier territory as I imagined Stevie completely naked, straddling my hips as we fucked, those full, firm tits jiggling as she bounced enthusiastically on my cock.

It wasn't the first time she'd starred in my illicit fantasies, and my neglected dick was completely on board with the idea, thickening in my slacks as another forbidden vision played through my mind, of pounding into her from behind, her silky hair wrapped tight around my fist. My fingers twitched as I envisioned pulling her head back and holding her in place as I drove deep into her pussy, her soft ass cushioning my driving thrusts as she moaned my name…

"Tell me you're having a good time."

The sound of Raven's voice over the music jolted me out of my depraved thoughts like a scratch on a vinyl record. My heart slammed hard in my chest. Jesus Christ. I hadn't even seen her approach or leave the dance floor, but then again, my gaze, my entire attention, had been riveted on Stevie, and my brain had been in the fucking gutter.

I cleared my throat as Raven plopped down onto the chair next to where I was sitting, the skirt of her champagne-colored dress settling over her legs. I tried to put the pieces of what she'd just said to me together, and failed. I didn't have a fucking clue what she'd asked me.

"What was that?" I asked in a casual tone. "I was distracted and didn't hear you."

"Clearly," she said with a little smirk on her lips, which made me wonder if she'd seen me ogling Stevie. "I said, tell me you're having a good time at my party."

"I'm having a good time at your party," I parroted.

She rolled her eyes, not amused. "And *mean* it.

"I *do* mean it," I said more genuinely, and finished off the bourbon in my glass.

Skepticism etched her pretty features and flickered in her green eyes. "You'd have a better time if you did something enjoyable for yourself for a change."

I arched a brow. "What's that supposed to mean?" I asked, even though I had a fair idea of where this conversation was heading.

"It means you focus on everything else to the exclusion of your own life, like work and Owen. Me, even."

I set my glass on the table beside me and smiled at her. "Those things *are* my life."

Her lips pursed, showing me that determined side to her personality. "And I'm here to tell you, from personal experience, it's not enough."

I arched a brow. "Oh, you're an expert now?"

"Yeah, I am." She nodded, crossing one leg over the other. "Remy showed me that there is much more to life than protecting your heart and emotions."

Raven had had every reason to do both for most of her life, and I was genuinely thrilled she'd found someone who cherished her the way she deserved.

I exhaled a deep breath and gave her a reassuring smile. "My heart and emotions are both doing just fine, thank you very much for your concern." Admittedly, though, both my heart and emotions had been through the wringer the past few years.

Another burst of laughter from Stevie, and my gaze instinctively drifted once again in that direction, watching as she now danced with our sister Cara, both of them bouncing on their feet with their hands waving in the air in time to the music. At some point Stevie had kicked her heels off, and as sexy as she'd looked with them on, I loved that she'd opted for comfort and didn't give a damn about decorum.

"Why don't you just ask her out already?"

I returned my attention to Raven, feigning confusion. "Who?" I asked.

Raven rolled her eyes, clearly not fooled. "Stevie, that's who. You've both been skirting around your attraction to one another since I introduced the two of you well over a year ago."

I shook my head. "Raven, the last thing I'm looking for is a relationship."

She laughed. "Who said anything about a relationship? You're both consenting adults, so why not just enjoy each other's company and have a good time together? That's what *dating* is."

"Because my life is shit right now?" I reminded her.

"My life was shit when Remy barged into it, remember?" she countered.

I winced because it was hard to forget how Lance had terrorized Raven, though I was grateful that Remy had become her savior, even when she'd tried to resist his protection.

The look in her eyes softened. "Look, all I'm saying is, work and everything else aside, you need to do things that make you feel good and make you happy. There is nothing wrong with that. It doesn't take away anything from Owen for you to enjoy someone else's company. You haven't dated anyone since filing for divorce and that was, what, two years ago?"

"Times flies," I quipped sarcastically.

She narrowed her gaze at me. "Don't be a jerk, Caleb."

I sighed and rubbed my palm along my jawline. "I'm not trying to be."

She reached out and touched my knee. "I just…want you to be happy."

I took her hand and gave it a reassuring squeeze. "Once this custody case over Owen is finalized, I'll be the happiest man around."

She frowned. "I hate that Alyssa is doing this to you. That joint custody of Owen isn't enough for her."

"You can't be surprised," I said, both of us well aware that Alyssa didn't really give a shit about how much time she spent with Owen. The custody suit had never been about that.

"No, I'm not surprised," she said, sounding sad. "Just disappointed that she'd use Owen as leverage to try and get back together with you, and if that doesn't work, then hurting you is no doubt her second option."

"Not gonna happen," I assured her.

"Good." Raven nodded succinctly. "You deserve so much better than what she's put you through."

"Hey, I've been looking for you, wife," Remy said, interrupting our discussion—thank God—as he strolled up to where we were sitting.

Raven's entire face lit up with adoration, and she grinned at her husband. "Ahh, the sound of that word, *wife*, never gets old."

"It better not," he said in a low, possessive growl that made me chuckle, and Raven blush. "Samantha and Dex are heading out and want to say their good-byes, so I'm stealing my *wife*," he said again.

Smiling and enjoying their dynamic, I waved a hand in the air. "She's all yours."

"Damn right she is." Remy extended his hand toward Raven, and she placed her own in his, allowing him to pull her up from the chair.

Raven glanced back at me. "Just think about what I said, okay?"

"Sure," I said, mostly to appease her.

After Remy and Raven walked away, I stood up, needing a breather after that conversation. I strolled over to the far side of the terrace, away from the party and where the music was more muted and the area provided some quiet and solitude.

The lighting didn't extend to this far corner of the rooftop, and it wasn't until I was in the secluded area that I realized someone else was already there, standing at the decorative stone balustrade that secured the perimeter and overlooked Manhattan. Stevie, to be exact, who looked to be texting someone on her phone, the light from the device the only thing illuminating her beautiful features and blonde hair.

"And here I thought I was the only one who needed a break from all the noise," I said as I approached her.

She jumped at the sound of my voice, obviously not expecting company. But as soon as she saw that it was me, she relaxed and smiled. "Yeah, I wanted to find someplace quiet to check in with my sister."

"She left already?" I asked, surprised. I hadn't noticed and assumed she'd been sitting at a table while Stevie was out on the dance floor.

Stevie nodded. "Yes, a while ago." She put her phone in her small purse, then set it on top of the wide stone wall before meeting my gaze in the shadows, caused by the reflection of the city's lights. "She's had a rough couple of weeks and I'm just worried about her."

I stood next to her at the railing. "Is everything okay?" I ventured to ask.

She exhaled a soft sigh. "I hope so? I mean, she's fine right now. She's assured me that she's in bed watching trashy reality TV but…well, she went through a bad breakup, one that required a restraining order against her abusive ex, and I'm just worried that the asshole isn't going to leave her alone. Narcissistic, entitled men like Mark don't like being put in their place."

I winced. "I'm sorry to hear that."

She nodded and gave me a murmured thanks. "It's just that I keep having flashbacks of the whole Lance thing with Raven and what an unhinged psycho he was…" Her words cut off and her eyes suddenly went wide. "Oh, shit. I'm so sorry. That was inappropriate."

I tipped my head, not the least bit offended. "Why? Because he's my twin brother? Trust me, I know who Lance is and it's not a solid, upstanding citizen. We were never close and we couldn't be more different."

"I just…" She shook her head, causing her soft blonde waves to brush across her shoulders. "I forget that he's your twin brother. The two of you don't look identical."

"No, we're fraternal, thank God."

She nodded, then leaned against the concrete railing and glanced out over the city. "So, where is Owen tonight?" she asked, making casual conversation.

"His mother has him for the weekend." I settled in beside her, arms braced on the top of the barrier. "I get him back tomorrow afternoon."

She gave me a curious, sidelong glance. "Is that hard…splitting time with her?"

"Always," I admitted. "It's too quiet when he's not around. I'm used to him running through the house no matter how many times I tell him not to, or playing his video games and the animated sounds he makes, or his constant inquisitive questions. Don't get me wrong. Having a bit of silence is nice, but I definitely feel like something is missing when he's gone."

"He's a great kid," she said softly, having interacted with him many times because of Raven being Owen's aunt. "He seems very well adjusted despite…"

Her voice trailed off again, as if she didn't want to broach a sensitive topic. "Despite the divorce and having to divide his time between two parents?" I finished for her.

"Yes." She smiled. "Every time I see the two of you together, he's like your little mini-me. Not only does he look a lot like you, at the pool party Raven and Remy had last month I was laughing at how much he tried to mimic you."

I vividly remembered that day, not because of my son's antics, but because of the bikini Stevie had worn that had her lush breasts and curves on display.

A light breeze blew, and I saw her shiver, and there was no missing the way her nipples tightened and pushed against the thin material of her dress. She rubbed her arms with her hands, and without thinking or even asking her if she was cold, because clearly she was and there were no heat lamps on this side of the terrace, I shrugged out of my suit coat.

"Here. Take my jacket," I said, settling the material

CARLY PHILLIPS & ERIKA WILDE

over her shoulders, not questioning the possessive way it made me feel to see her wrapped up in my coat.

She groaned as the warmth inside of the jacket chased away her chill. "So much better. Thank you." She grabbed the lapels and pulled them closed in front of her, and I watched as she put her nose against the expensive cashmere fabric, closed her eyes, and inhaled.

"Mmm." Her lashes drifted back open, her eyes half-mast and flirtatious. "It smells like you."

I cocked my head, though my dick reacted to the husky tone of her voice. "Is that a good thing?"

"A *really* good thing." She breathed in the scent again, and I imagined her doing the same thing against my neck where I'd lightly sprayed the fragrance. "Whatever cologne you wear…now *that's* an aphrodisiac."

I chuckled. "Better than oysters?"

She laughed. "Most definitely."

We both turned back to the stunning view of Manhattan at night, a comfortable silence settling between us.

I was the first to break it. "So, I've always been curious," I said, casting a glance her way. "Is Stevie short for another name, like Stephanie?"

"No," she said, and gave a wry laugh as she turned her head to look at me. "I'm actually lucky my name isn't *Steven*. My father wanted a son. He didn't get one with Valerie, who my mother named. And when I was born a girl, out of pure spite he named me Stevie, since that was the name he'd picked out for a boy."

I felt my brows rise in shock.

"Yes, my father was an asshole," she said bitterly, giving me the impression that her family's history was just as dysfunctional as my own.

I didn't want her traveling down that road. Not tonight, when everything was so enjoyable between us. "I like the name. It suits you."

She gave me a skeptical, challenging look. "How so?"

"You're feisty. Fun. Easygoing." Without thinking, I lifted a hand and brushed a few wayward strands of hair off her cheek, the pads of my fingers caressing her soft skin. "Maybe even creative or artistic. Adventurous, despite not trying oysters."

Her lips parted as she stared into my eyes, captivating me. "I wouldn't have thought you'd paid that much attention to me, to be able to come to that conclusion."

"Stevie…I paid attention." My voice was low, raspier than I'd intended. I wanted to tell her all the things I'd noticed, all the different ways I'd imagined kissing her, fucking her, hearing her soft, sultry moans as I made her come.

Our eyes remained locked, and in the background I vaguely heard the DJ announce the last song of the evening. In front of me, Stevie's pink, glossy lips curled up in a mischievous smile.

"Last song of the night and it's a slow one," she mused playfully. "Care to dance?"

I recognized a dare when I saw one. A temptation I ought to resist, but Raven was right. I did need to do things that made me feel good and happy, and right now, Stevie tapped into both.

Without verbally replying, I closed the short distance between us and took her into my arms. Sliding one arm inside my jacket and around her waist to bring our bodies flush together, and taking hold of her hand in mine. I heard her soft gasp of surprise, which reflected in her eyes as she looked up at me, as if she hadn't really thought I'd follow through on her challenge.

We were quiet as we slow danced in the dark, our bodies moving in sync, neither one of us breaking eye contact. Our thighs rubbed as we shifted, and I slid my hand lower, to the base of her spine. Splaying my fingers, I pressed her even tighter against me, making sure she could feel the hard ridge of my cock grinding against her stomach.

Having her this close was pure torture, considering all the wicked things I'd already done to her in my head, in my dirtiest fantasies when I was alone at night, dick in hand. As the sexual tension between us heightened, I decided that tonight I wasn't going to fight the attraction between us.

Mutual desire flickered in her gaze and her tongue skimmed her lower lip. "Caleb…" she whispered.

I heard the soft plea in her voice, and wanting to selfishly indulge myself when it came to Stevie, I released her hand and pushed my fingers through her hair, gripping the soft strands and tipping her head back so that her mouth was right below mine. Without hesitation, I crushed my lips to hers. Seconds later, my tongue slid deep and tangled with hers. She clutched the front of my shirt in her hands and whimpered, the needy sound reverberating throughout my entire body.

God, she made me fucking ravenous.

I thought I could stop with one taste, but I was wrong. Her mouth molded to mine as the kiss turned deeper, hotter, both of us unable to get enough. All I could think about was stripping her bare, licking her *everywhere*, then sinking as deep as I could get inside her pussy.

My dick throbbed at the thought, and judging by the way she arched against me and made soft mewling sounds, there was no denying she wanted the same thing.

Knowing that our make-out session was about to get out of hand in a very public place, and quickly, I ended the kiss. My hand was still in her hair, and she looked dazed by what had just transpired between us. Right now, all I wanted was this one thing: a night with Stevie, just for myself. Desperately.

"Come back to my place," I whispered, issuing the invitation as I slid my palm down so that I was cupping her cheek and my thumb slid across her damp bottom lip. "I don't have pomegranates, but I do have chocolate."

A sparkle lit her eyes, and she smiled at my teasing comment. "That's okay with me, because I hate pomegranates."

I chuckled. "I'll add that to your list of things you won't eat."

She bit her bottom lip, looking adorably sexy. "And, Caleb, you don't need chocolate to seduce me. You already have."

CHAPTER THREE

Stevie

M Y ENTIRE BODY buzzed as Caleb and I separated to say our goodbyes to everyone so it wasn't blatantly obvious that we were leaving together. Raven might be my best friend, but I decided there was no need for her to know that I was hooking up with her brother, considering I was pretty sure this was just a one-night thing. If it turned into something more, well, then I'd have that conversation with her.

But for now, sneaking off with Caleb felt so sexy and illicit, and I had to admit I liked the feeling of being whisked away by the one man who'd starred in my fantasies the past year. I couldn't wait to see how the evening played out, but I was already filled with the anticipation of finally scratching this itch between us.

As we'd agreed, I met Caleb in the lobby of the hotel after we both bid our farewells. I'd given him his jacket back once we'd made the decision to leave the party individually, but he hadn't put it back on. It was still draped over his arm, and as soon as I reached him he put it back around my shoulders to keep me warm.

There was something about the sweet, almost romantic gesture that gave me *all* the feels, even as I cautioned myself to not let foolish notions play out in my head. This wasn't a relationship. Hell, this wasn't even a date. It was just pleasure for the sake of pleasure, two consenting adults enjoying an intense sexual attraction for a night, and I told myself I was okay with that.

A luxury SUV was waiting at the curb as we walked outside—not an Uber but what appeared to be Caleb's own private car with a driver named Dylan. Once we were settled in the back seat and Caleb directed the driver to his place, The Cortland in West Chelsea, I withdrew my phone from my purse and typed out a text to Valerie.

Okay, you win. I'm spending a little extra time with Caleb tonight, if you know what I mean. I added a grinning emoji and sent off the message.

You lucky girl! Enjoy the night, Caleb, and hopefully multiple orgasms. She followed that up with five fireworks emojis.

I groaned and shook my head to myself.

"Everything okay?" Caleb asked.

He'd insisted I sit beside him in the back seat, and I turned my head to look up at his handsome face, backlit by the city lights outside the tinted windows. "Just letting my sister know I won't be home for a few more hours."

He flashed a wicked grin that made my panties

immediately damp. "A few more hours?" he murmured as he placed a hand right above my bare knee, his fingers hot on my cool skin as they curved possessively around my lower thigh. "Tell her you won't be home until mid-morning."

The fact that he wanted me to spend the night at his place surprised me. "Are you sure about that?"

"Absolutely." His hand stroked a little higher, stopping at the hem of my dress and making me all too aware of his touch...and wishing it would traverse *all* the way up my thigh. "I plan to make the most of our night together, and our morning, which includes breakfast." He winked at me.

It was an offer I found impossible to resist, not to mention this charming side to Caleb's personality. I shot off a quick text to let Valerie know this newest change of plans, then put my phone in my purse so I didn't have to see her reply to *that*. Then, I glanced out the window, taking in the scenery as we made our way to the west side of Manhattan.

"This area is...well, very nice," I said, making conversation. "I've never really ventured to this part of the city." For a reason. Because everything, from housing to restaurants to shopping, were out of my budget and a girl like me didn't belong here. Hell, just breathing the air in this neighborhood probably cost a premium.

"How long have you lived in New York?" he asked, his tone curious as we slowly made our way through Saturday evening traffic.

I shifted my gaze back to his. "Almost three years

now."

He considered that for a moment. "Where did you move from?"

Again, his tone was casual and inquisitive. I would have chalked up his questions to small talk to fill the time until we reached his place, but he looked genuinely interested in my answers, which made it easy to share that part of myself with him. "A very small town in Connecticut, where I grew up."

He tipped his head, his thumb rubbing absently along my inner thigh. "And what made you move here, of all places?"

I shrugged and replied honestly. "Both Valerie and I needed a change." An understatement considering what we'd left behind. A mother who'd been murdered at the hands of our father, and our father in prison serving a life sentence for the crime. Not the kind of sordid background I wanted to share with a man like Caleb. And there was no reason to, considering this was just one night together.

I gave him a smile. "New York City seemed exciting and filled with possibilities."

He chuckled. "So people say. And your parents? They still live there?"

I paused, then decided to reframe the truth. "Unfortunately, they're both gone," I said, which was honestly my reality. My father, to me, was as good as dead.

"I'm sorry to hear that," he replied, compassion in his tone.

"Thank you," I murmured, not sure what else to say, but was saved by making further conversation about my parents as the SUV turned, then circled into a valet area under a building.

"Here you are, sir," his driver announced.

"Thank you, Dylan," Caleb said as he unbuckled his seat belt, then reached over to my far hip and unclasped mine, bringing our faces close together. "Are you good?" he asked me.

I appreciated his concern, and I knew his question left the door open for me to change my mind about spending the night, but an evening of mindless pleasure was exactly what I wanted, and needed.

"Yeah, I'm good," I said, and smiled. "So long as you promise to make me *feel* good."

He grinned. "No worries about that, sweetheart," he said in deep, husky tones that made me shiver in anticipation. "I'm going to redefine the words 'feel good' for you all night long."

I laughed flirtatiously, ready to enjoy whatever this man wanted to do with and to me. "Then what are we waiting for?"

We got out of the car, and Caleb slipped his hand in mine as we walked into the lobby of the upscale complex. I immediately felt out of my element surrounded by such opulence, and there was no missing the speculative glances of a few women we passed that eyed me like they knew I was an imposter. My face flushed, because I was well aware that I was no match for their sophistication, or the flashy, designer hand-

CARLY PHILLIPS & ERIKA WILDE

bags and clothes they wore compared to my polyester dress and worn heels—and they knew it, too. Hell, they probably thought I was a call girl because it was clear I did not belong in this part of the city.

Caleb either didn't notice the stares, or didn't care as he greeted the man at the front desk we passed on our way to the elevator. Once we stepped into the lift and he swiped a key card, the door shut and the smooth ride upward began.

He turned toward me, his perceptive gaze taking in my features and clearly seeing my unease. "Are you okay?"

"I'm just a little overwhelmed by…everything," I said, sweeping a hand around us to indicate the interior of the elevator, which was just as posh as the rest of the building with a marbled floor, the walls in a rich, polished wood, and gold accents that gleamed. "And a little intimidated, if I'm being honest."

"You have no reason to be either." He stepped closer and framed my face in his hands, a sinful smile tipping up the corners of his mouth. "But clearly, you need a distraction because I want your mind thinking about only one thing. Tonight is about me and you and nothing else."

His mouth descended on mine, and seconds later I was lost in his quick and dirty kiss that erased everything from my head but the taste and feel of his body against mine, and the effortless way he made me forget everything but him. His tongue delved deep, his teeth grazed along my lower lip, then gently bit, drawing a moan from deep in my throat. By the time the doors slid open and he lifted his mouth from mine, I was dizzy, thoroughly aroused, and clinging to him.

Satisfaction etched his features. "Perfect," he murmured, then grabbed my hand once more and led me out of the elevator.

I expected a hallway that would lead to his apartment door, but we walked directly into his luxurious penthouse. The place was like a damn palace. A foyer led to an open-concept area with high ceilings, a spacious living room, and a kitchen off to the side. As we entered, a lamp automatically flicked on, a soft glow of light revealing an interior that was decorated in navy blue and cream colors and accented in gold. For a man who had a six-year-old son, the place was immaculate.

Drawn to the floor-to-ceiling windows overlooking the city, I slipped out of my heels and draped the jacket I was still wearing over the back of a leather chair, then walked in that direction, impressed and awed because this was a level of wealthy I was unfamiliar with. The glittering nighttime cityscape was jaw-dropping and breathtaking, along with a waterfront view of the Hudson River.

"Care for something to drink?" Caleb asked.

I glanced back at him, watching as he tugged his tie off, then unbuttoned his cuffs and rolled up his sleeves, making himself comfortable. "No, I'm good. Thank you."

I returned my stare out the windows. "This view is

spectacular."

I heard him walk up behind me and my heart rate accelerated when he pushed all my hair over one shoulder, leaving the other side of my neck bare. I shivered as he placed a warm, damp kiss just below my ear, his breath fanning across my skin. "I'm far more interested in a whole different kind of view, but you go ahead and enjoy the city while I enjoy *you*."

I *tried* to focus on the glittering city lights as he slowly unzipped my dress, his fingers trailing along my spine as the material parted, all the way down to my hips. He pushed the fabric off my shoulders, and I watched my reflection in the window as the dress slithered down my body to pool around my feet, leaving me in a cream-colored lace bra and panties, while he was still fully clothed.

He unfastened the hooks on my bra, and even though my first instinct was to hold it in place to keep myself covered, I allowed him to push the lingerie off my arms and expose my breasts.

"Can anyone see in?" I asked, not sure how I felt with my body on display.

His big hands came around, cupping my breasts and fondling them. "Would it bother you if they could?"

I gasped as he plucked my stiff, aching nipples, jolting my entire body with that shock of pleasure. "Yes…no," I whispered, momentarily confused.

"You have a gorgeous body any man would love to watch," he said in a husky voice as one of his hands left my breast and skimmed down along my stomach. "But if it makes you feel better, there is a privacy film on the windows. At night you can see out, but no one can see in, so relax and enjoy what I'm about to do to you."

He didn't make me wait long to show me what he intended. My breathing escalated in anticipation as his hand dipped into the waistband of my panties and down between my legs where I was slick and needy. I whimpered as he grazed my sensitive clit, and he groaned in my ear as his fingers sank into my pussy.

"Jesus, you're so fucking wet for me," he growled, sliding deeper.

His fingers continued to expertly stroke me—too light to make me come, much to my frustration.

"The other nice thing about those windows at night, I can also see your reflection while I'm playing with your tits, and my other hand is pleasuring your pussy, and that's so fucking hot."

He tugged on a nipple, and I moaned, my head falling back on his shoulder as my hips bucked against his hand.

"Do you know what would be even hotter?" he murmured.

"What?" I whispered, wanting to know.

"Pushing you up against that window and fucking you from behind."

My sex clenched at the image that flashed through my mind, and he chuckled in my ear. "Oh, yeah, you like that idea, don't you?"

I did. Too much. Who knew beneath those power suits that Caleb wore that he was absolutely filthy and depraved when it came to sex?

I rolled my hips, trying to increase the pressure and friction of his fingers against my clit. "Caleb…please," I begged, desperate for the orgasm he was holding just out of my reach.

"Please what?" he teased.

I didn't censor my words. "Let me come."

He continued those slow, lazy, too gentle strokes across my needy flesh. "Show me how badly you want it."

Shedding every last inhibition, I slid a hand into my panties to join his, pressing his fingers harder against my clit, forcing him to increase the rhythm and friction just the way I needed. He lowered his other arm, wrapping it tight around my waist and hauling me right up against the front of his body, as if he was getting ready to completely unravel every part of me and I'd need the extra support of him holding me upright.

So many wild, intense sensations crashed through me, and I closed my eyes to savor them all and enjoy Caleb's expertise. My arm reached up so that I could slide my hand through his soft, thick hair, gripping the strands as I shamelessly fucked his fingers.

My hips rolled and bucked, thrusting against the hand in my panties then rocking back to rub against the solid length of his erection, a hard pillar of flesh that made my core clench at the thought of him burying all those inches deep inside of me.

He growled against the side of my neck, the sound making me shiver. "Look at you," he ordered, and I pried my eyes open to obey. "So fucking beautiful. Grinding against my hand, your ass pushing so eagerly against my cock. Come for me, Stevie."

My reflection in the window showed me every-thing. Had I ever acted so wanton before? *Never,* but then I'd never been with a confident, sexually assured man like Caleb.

That elusive feeling of being desired completely consumed me, pushing me over the edge and into a powerful orgasm that seemed to spiral me into a whole other dimension. I cried out, vaguely hearing Caleb murmuring words of encouragement and praise as my body quivered and my climax left me breathless and boneless.

I slumped back against him, grateful for the arm he'd anchored around my waist that kept me from collapsing to the floor. My head was still tilted back and resting on his shoulder as I tried to regain my equilibrium, and in the window's reflection I watched as he withdrew his hand from my panties and brought it up to his mouth, sucking the taste of me off of his fingers.

He groaned, as if he'd just enjoyed a rare delicacy. "Jesus, I knew you'd taste so fucking good."

The fact that he'd imagined *tasting me* made me lightheaded.

He dropped his hand down to my hip and nuzzled

my neck. "You ready to take this to the bedroom so I can fuck you properly, on a bed?"

"Oh, now you're being all formal," I teased, and he chuckled. "I don't think my shaking legs are capable of getting me there."

"Then allow me," he said, and swept me up into his arms.

CHAPTER FOUR

Stevie

I LET OUT a startled squeal, my hands grasping onto Caleb's shoulders as my feet left the floor and I found myself cradled against his chest. Even though I wasn't a petite woman, I couldn't bring myself to protest because the effortless way he carried me was so damn sexy. So I held on for the ride as he headed down a long hallway, passing several rooms until he reached an obscenely large bedroom.

As soon as we entered, one of the lamps at the side of the bed automatically flicked on, giving me a glimpse of more floor-to-ceiling windows and navy and cream décor and dark wood furniture. He set me down on the king-size bed and walked away, unbuttoning his dress shirt.

"I want your panties off by the time I get back, which gives you all of ten seconds," he ordered, disappearing into what looked to be the en suite.

I reclined back against the soft pillows, and he returned in five, before I had the chance to comply. He tossed a strip of four condoms onto the mattress and shrugged out of his shirt, distracting me with a glimpse of his toned chest and firm, lickable abs.

He snapped his fingers to get my attention, and I redirected my eyes back up to his face. "Are you looking to get spanked?" he asked, and I caught the playful look in his eyes, though I wasn't opposed to feeling his hand smacking my ass.

"No, sir," I replied impudently.

He smirked as he slowly unbuckled his slim leather belt, then opened his dress pants, frazzling my brains all over again as I anxiously awaited the strip show so I could finally see what he was packing—something impressive judging by the long, thick erection straining against the fabric of his pants.

"Panties off, Stevie. Now," he repeated in a firm, gruff tone.

I quickly removed my underwear and tossed them aside.

He stood at the foot of the bed, his slacks unzipped, but still on. "Spread your legs for me."

I arched a brow and kept my knees pressed primly together, just to see what he would do. "Bossy much?"

His gaze narrowed, but it was the predatory look in his eyes that should have warned me. "Bossy *and* impatient to see what's mine for the night."

He reached out and grabbed my ankles, and I exhaled a squeak of surprise as he dragged me all the way down to the foot of the bed, until my ass was on the edge of the mattress and my thighs were forced to spread open around his hips.

He gave me a satisfied smile as he looked his fill of my pussy. "*Much* better," he said, quickly removing the last of his clothes and kicking them aside before resuming his position between my legs.

His eyes were dark and hot as he ran his fingers through my drenched slit. "This view of your body while I fuck you is far superior, anyway. I can see everything. The bounce of your breasts as I thrust into you, the way your pussy is going to take every inch of my cock."

I groaned, his dirty talk turning me on even more.

Completely, gloriously naked, he took his erect shaft in his hand, stroking the length and sliding his palm up over the crown, then squeezing the tip. If I wasn't so desperate to feel him deep inside of me, I would have been on my hands and knees in front of him, eagerly sucking him off. Hopefully I'd get that chance…later.

Reaching for one of the foil packets, he tore it open and rolled the condom down his length. "Bend your knees back."

This time I did so without hesitation, offering myself to him.

"Good girl," he said, that seductive praise making me go all soft and gooey inside for pleasing him.

He dragged the head of his cock from my sensitive clit all the way down to my entrance, notching the crown there. Slowly, inevitably, he pushed his way inside, his eyes watching as his length gradually disappeared inside my body.

A groan escaped his lips, his expression infused with pleasure when he finally bottomed out inside me. "That first fucking stroke is *everything*," he rasped. "You feel incredible. So warm and tight around my cock."

Our bodies were joined but he didn't move. I didn't think I'd ever felt so stretched, so full, so *needy*. It was all too much, and yet not enough.

"Caleb," I moaned, gripping the bed covers and clenching my internal muscles around his shaft. "I need you to fuck me."

"I'm getting there," he promised, draping my legs over his arms to keep them spread wide. He leaned forward just enough to grip my waist with his hands, pinning my hips to the mattress so he was in control. "Just savoring the moment, and you."

My breath caught at those words. "Savor me a little faster, please."

"So impatient and demanding." His eyes danced with humor as he leisurely started to move, giving me too short, unhurried thrusts. Pulling out a few inches at a time, then back in, teasing and tormenting me.

"More," I begged, arching my back and trying to lift my hips to speed things up, but my lower body was his to command. "Harder...faster...*deeper*."

"Such a greedy girl," he murmured, though he gradually increased his rhythm, giving me the deep penetration and friction I craved.

I gasped as he slammed into me, both of us groaning as that restraint of his slipped. I bit my bottom lip, staring up at him. He'd told me he liked this position, of me spread open for him, taking his cock while he watched…but I also liked my view of him. His broad, defined chest. Those stomach muscles that bunched every time he drove into me. The way his jaw clenched as he tried to remain in control. The way his eyes glazed over with lust as he finally gave himself over to the need to rut because fucking me felt *that* good.

But still, he maintained that control I was determined to shatter.

Still holding me down and open for him, I moved one of my hands, trailing my fingers down my stomach as his hot, hungry gaze tracked where I was headed. I rubbed my clit, hard and fast, and with his cock driving in and out of me, it didn't take long for my orgasm to crest. I rode the blissful wave, my head falling back and inarticulate sounds filling the room while my pussy pulsed around Caleb's shaft, milking him, forcing him to give in to his own release, which had been my goal.

He swore beneath his breath as he slammed into me one last time, his entire body stiffening as he came inside of me, long and hard.

AFTER OUR THIRD round of sexual aerobics, I collapsed onto the bed on my stomach with a sated sigh, my dry spell officially over. Jesus, the man was a beast in the bedroom, fucking me three times in the past hour, all in different ways. I was going to be sore tomorrow, but I'd at least go home with a smile on my face from all the generous orgasms.

My body still vibrated with pleasure from the last one, and when I turned my head on the pillow and met Caleb's gaze beside me, he gave me a smirk that held more than a little bit of arrogance. I couldn't begrudge him that smug attitude. He'd earned it. His big dick energy definitely extended to the bedroom.

He rolled to his side, propped his head up with his hand, and lightly skimmed his finger down my spine, making me shiver from that touch…until he reached my ass and gave it a playful smack.

I gasped at the slight sting, looking affronted when I was anything but. "Hey, what was that for?"

"Because I know you secretly wanted me to spank you that first time when you didn't take off your panties like I told you to."

I gave him a sassy grin. "Guilty."

"And maybe the second time, too, when you took your sweet time getting on your hands and knees for me. I should have smacked your ass right then and there, but I was more interested in *tapping* that ass."

I laughed. "I have to say, your recovery time is impressive," I teased him.

Shockingly, there hadn't been much downtime on his part between each orgasm, though he had used those brief respites to do wicked things to my body with his mouth and hands, which had clearly aroused him all over again.

He caressed the sting on my bottom with his hand, his eyes holding mine. "If I'm being honest, it's been a while. I've got a lot to make up for."

Surprise rippled through me, because I couldn't imagine a virile man like Caleb depriving himself of those pleasures. "How long?" I asked curiously.

He hesitated a moment. "A year."

My jaw dropped open in shock, and he chuckled and pushed my mouth shut. "Dating hasn't been a priority with work, Owen, and this custody case hanging over my head and Alyssa scrutinizing everything I do to use it to her advantage. And I'm not the type to troll bars or dating apps for a quick lay with a stranger. It's not my style."

Which made our night together...*special*? My traitorous heart skipped a beat, and I immediately dismissed that fanciful thought, even if our time together had been amazing thus far. But that's all this was, I reminded myself. One night. No promises or expectations of anything more.

But it was rare to find a man in his prime who didn't seek female company, for the sole purpose of sexual release. It was actually refreshing. "It's not my style, either," I told him.

I'd always strived for meaningful relationships when it came to physical intimacy, and not casual sex for the sake of it. It was even difficult to define tonight with Caleb as *casual*, not when I really liked him on a personal level and it already felt as though we'd developed a more meaningful connection that had nothing to do with sex.

A smile lifted the corner of his mouth as he tucked a disheveled strand of hair behind my ear, his touch sweet and tender. "So, if my recovery time is impressive, it's because I want tonight with you, and every orgasm, to count."

Well, okay then.

That *one night* was hammered home again. Disappointing, but I understood and respected his reasons. Especially considering he'd just told me that his ex-wife scrutinized everything he did during their ongoing custody suit. Which had to be exhausting, emotionally and mentally. That couldn't be easy to deal with.

Abruptly, he moved off the bed and stood. "I'll be right back," he said, then disappeared into the bathroom where I heard him cleaning up. But when he came back out—still naked—instead of rejoining me he walked out of the bedroom, giving me a great view of his bare, muscular ass as he left.

I heard him doing something down the hall in the kitchen, the sound of drawers opening and closing and something like glass being set on the counter. Figuring he was probably getting a snack, I snuggled under the weight of the softest, most luxurious comforter I'd ever been wrapped up in.

My eyes had just drifted shut when Caleb returned.

"Sit up against the pillows," he said when he saw me huddled beneath the covers.

I made a grumpy sound. "I was just getting comfortable...and sleepy," I admitted. "You wore me out."

"Already?" He chuckled. "You're a lightweight, and I'm not done with you yet."

I arched a brow at him, but begrudgingly scooted back up, propping myself against the headboard, the covers falling to my lap as he settled beside me.

I looked at the small, decorative glass dish in his hand, confused by the swirl of brown stuff inside. "What's that?"

"Chocolate, of course, which I promised you," he said, reminding me of our aphrodisiac conversation. He dragged a spoon through the treat and waggled his brows at me. "We've got a long night ahead of us, so open up."

I couldn't resist that mischievous light in his eyes, or the temptation of chocolate, and I did as I was told, accepting the mouthful of…the lightest, most decadent chocolate mousse to ever pass my lips.

I closed my eyes and moaned, the sound similar as to when Caleb made me orgasm. "Oh, my God," I said, knowing I was probably giving him a swoony look, and it wasn't for him, but the mousse. "Where did this magically come from?"

He grinned. "My chef made it."

Of course he had a personal chef.

He dipped the spoon back into the confection. "It's one of Owen's favorites, and since he'll be home tomorrow Marcel made a batch."

"So I'm stealing one of Owen's desserts?" I almost didn't care, it was that good.

"He'll never know," Caleb said, winking at me.

He fed me a few more bites, grinning as I continued to moan and groan blissfully.

"I take it the aphrodisiac is working?"

"Maybe." I licked a smear of chocolate off my bottom lip and watched his eyes darken as he tracked the movement of my tongue. "You might have to be more persuasive."

"Hmm." He made the thoughtful sound as he scooped up another serving, but as he lifted it to my mouth, he deliberately tipped the spoon and the dollop plopped onto my bare breast. I gasped, because it was cold and unexpected.

He gave me a depraved grin. "Whoops. Clumsy me." He set the dish and spoon on the nightstand next to his side of the bed. "Let me clean that up."

His index finger reached toward my breast, and I thought he'd swipe up the mousse, but instead he smeared it all over my nipple, then down my stomach, painting my skin with the sticky chocolate.

I sucked in another shocked breath, desire already running through my veins, because I knew where this was heading. "*Caleb.*"

"My turn for dessert," he said huskily and dipped his head, latching onto my nipple.

He sucked the sensitive tip, arousal flooding my body as he swirled and flicked his tongue over and around the crest, then tugged with his teeth. A soft whimper escaped my lips, and I threaded my fingers through his hair, gripping the strands as he licked his way lower, cleaning up the mess he'd made on my stomach.

My brain felt as though it was about to short-circuit from all the pleasure. One of his hands slid between my legs, long fingers gliding along my slit. I could feel how slick he'd made me. Again.

He looked up at me with a smirk. "Look at that. Feeding you chocolate worked," he murmured.

I wanted to argue that it had nothing to do with the dessert and everything to do with him, but he rolled to his back, grabbing my waist and positioning me so that I was sitting astride his thighs and his semi-erect shaft was right in front of me. He reached for a foil packet on the nightstand and handed it to me.

"Put it on me while I watch," he said.

Sheathing a dick with a condom wasn't something I was adept at, but I was always up for a challenge and it didn't take me long to realize why he'd assigned me the chore. Because touching him, grasping his cock to hold it still while I positioned the latex over the head then rolled it all the way down his length, made him rock hard. By the time I was done, his rigid cock was engorged and pointed at the ceiling, ready for action.

His dark eyes met mine, daring me. "Straddle my cock and ride me, Stevie."

Biting my bottom lip, I scooted up and positioned myself over him, then oh-so slowly sank down on his shaft, taking him all the way inside me until I was stretched full. I loved the way he shuddered in pleasure beneath me, loved even more the deep growl that reverberated in his chest as my internal muscles clenched tight around him.

With his hands gripping my waist and his gaze on mine, I began to move, determined to make the most of the rest of the night with him. Because that was all I could ever have with Caleb Kane.

CHAPTER FIVE

Caleb

I STOOD IN the kitchen, beating half a dozen eggs for the breakfast I'd promised Stevie while she finished taking a shower. After our night together, and how much energy and calories we'd undoubtedly burned, I was ravenous for food and I was sure she was as well.

I was also in a great mood and knew Stevie was the reason, and the fantastic sex was only a small contribution to my cheerful disposition. I couldn't remember the last time I'd enjoyed a woman's company so much, our natural, effortless connection making it so easy for me to relax and forget about my troubles, if only for a little while.

It was as though Stevie was the hit of dopamine I needed to chase away the stress of the things in my life that felt unsettled and had kept me so uptight and serious since my divorce. Her lack of pretense was so appealing when I lived in a world where genuine connections seemed rare, buried under layers of expectations and superficial facades. Her playful personality lightened me up, and I was drawn to her upbeat attitude despite the hard things she'd endured in her own life.

For the first time in what seemed like forever, I felt like I was turning a corner in my personal life. That after last night with Stevie, between our connection and our chemistry, I was ready to open myself up to the possibility of dating seriously again. And not just anyone, but Stevie. Because Raven was right. I'd spent the past two years focusing on everything else to the exclusion of my own wants and needs, and maybe it was time to do something that made *me* happy for a change.

Stevie, I realized, made me very happy. Even now, just thinking of her and how well we'd clicked on so many different levels, how much she'd made me laugh and *feel* more than just mundane emotions, I had a goofy grin on my face. I could feel a few of my walls crumbling, that guard I was so used to maintaining falling to the wayside to let her in. I never thought I'd be able to get to a place in my life where I'd feel optimistic about the future again, but Stevie had changed my mindset.

Dating Stevie would certainly be a balancing act, considering the upcoming custody hearing for Owen, and Alyssa looking for any reason to create conflict. But I wasn't ready to let Stevie walk away without exploring the possibilities, or to let our one night together be nothing more than that.

Those thoughts tumbled through my mind as I continued prepping everything for our breakfast, using the fresh mushrooms and chopped ham Marcel had left in the refrigerator. I sauteed them together, and just as they were done Stevie padded into the kitchen.

I turned off the stove and set the pan on a back burner, taking a moment to appreciate the way she filled out one of my T-shirts I'd given her to wear so she didn't have to put her dress back on until she was ready to head home. It hung to mid-thigh, lightly skimming her curves and her full, unbound breasts. Her perky nipples poked against the fabric and made my dick twitch in my sweatpants.

The ends of her wavy blonde hair were damp and she'd washed the last of her makeup off in the shower, leaving her fresh-faced, which I found incredibly appealing because I could see the genuine flush of color on her cheeks.

She was a natural beauty, and even stripped down to basics I liked that she seemed comfortable in her own skin. It was a rare kind of confidence I found attractive and sexy. She wasn't worried about trying to impress me or attempting to hide behind external trappings. Then again, after all the ways I'd fucked her during the course of the night, seeing and touching every inch of her, there was nothing left to hide from me.

"What?" she asked, looking around the kitchen wide-eyed and disappointed. "No personal chef this morning?"

I saw the teasing glimmer in her eyes and smiled at her. "Just because I employ a chef doesn't mean I can't cook. In fact, it's something I enjoy but with my hours at the office, it's easier to have well-balanced meals prepped for Owen."

She glanced over at the stove, seeing the mushrooms and ham I'd already sauteed. "I'm impressed."

Then, she sauntered over to me barefoot. Stopping in front of where I was standing, she lifted up on her tiptoes and brushed her lips softly across mine, no morning-after awkwardness for her. "Thank you for last night, and earlier this morning, and all the amazing orgasms," she said, grinning playfully. "You've made my kitty very happy."

I chuckled at her euphemism, and just as she attempted to step away, I wrapped an arm around her waist and brought her body flush to mine. "How about I make your kitty purr one more time before breakfast?"

I only had a few more hours before Alyssa dropped Owen off, and I wanted to enjoy every last moment with Stevie before reality intruded. Backing her against the granite island in the middle of the kitchen, I grabbed her waist and lifted her so she was sitting on the surface.

"Seriously, how do you have any stamina left?" she asked, already sounding breathless as I moved to stand in between her parted knees, her pussy perfectly aligned with my stiffening dick as soon as I removed her panties and shoved my sweatpants down.

"All I have to do is look at you, at the nipples poking against my shirt and those red marks I left on your neck from my morning stubble, and I get hard." I gave her a wicked grin. "I like the thought of leaving those same abrasions between your thighs so you'll think of me later, every time you walk and feel that slight chafe and burn."

Her lashes fell half-mast, desire infusing her expression. "You just want to leave your mark *everywhere.*"

"Damn right I do," I growled, not questioning the surge of possessiveness I felt when it came to her. I wanted her to leave here today looking well and truly fucked by me, with the memorable marks to prove it.

She rolled her eyes playfully, her hand lifting up and sliding along my prickly, unshaven jaw. "You're such a typical man."

But she wasn't complaining, nor did she protest when I pushed my fingers into her hair and crushed my mouth to hers. With a soft moan, her lips automatically parted beneath the onslaught of mine and I slid my tongue inside, tasting the minty toothpaste I'd left out for her on the bathroom counter, along with a new toothbrush.

I dropped a palm to her knee, sliding it upward, and she made a soft, mewling sound of need as her hands stroked down my chest, along my stomach, and reached the waistband of my sweatpants.

In the back of my mind, an odd noise in the foyer barely registered through the lust fogging my brain…until I heard the sound of running feet. Confused, I jerked back, ending the kiss with Stevie as I tried to make sense of what was happening while watching Owen zoom past the other side of the kitchen island, heading toward the hallway with his backpack slung over his shoulder.

"Hey, Dad!" he said, raising a hand up in a quick wave.

Owen didn't stop, didn't even glance my way, his focus on getting to his bedroom so he could play on his Xbox, which was how every drop-off went. A six-year-old whose only care in the world was immersing himself in his favorite video game that Alyssa didn't allow him to play when he was with her.

Normally, I would have called out to Owen to not run in the house, or even ordered him to come back and give me a hug after being gone for the week, but today I let him go, grateful that he'd remain oblivious to the awkward situation I'd found myself in with Stevie.

"Seriously, Caleb," Alyssa said, her tone dripping with disgust as she walked into the kitchen and stopped on the other side of the island. "You openly fuck a woman in your kitchen on the day that your son is expected back home? I guess Cece was right about seeing you with a two-bit whore in the lobby last night," she said of one of her friends who also lived in the building.

I flinched at her crass words and heard Stevie suck in a quick breath. Fury was right on the heels of that vulgar remark. I couldn't even deal with or acknowledge my ex right now, though I had plenty to say in response. My only concern was for Stevie, who was still sitting on the counter in front of me in a very compromising position. I looked down at her, her eyes wide with distress as I watched the play of emotions flit across her face.

Her initial shock gave way to panic and mortification as she stared up at me. "I…uh, should leave you two to…talk."

"Yes, you should," Alyssa said in a haughty tone. "Caleb and I clearly have a lot to discuss."

I wanted to tell Alyssa to shut the fuck up, that I didn't need her unsolicited comments, but I wasn't going to engage with her in front of Stevie. That was the last thing I wanted her to witness when I knew how vicious Alyssa could be. The best thing to do was to put Stevie in a safe place until I dealt with my ex.

I helped Stevie off of the counter, hating how tense her entire body was, along with that flush on her cheeks that had nothing to do with desire and everything to do with embarrassment.

I glanced at Alyssa, the smug look on her face pissing me off even more. "I'll be back," I said tersely.

She flashed me an almost triumphant smile. "I'll be waiting."

"Come on," I said to Stevie, and with a hand at her back, I guided her down the hall until we were in my bedroom.

Once we were there, I turned her around to face me and curved my hands around the side of her neck. She wouldn't look at me, so I used my thumbs to tip her chin back, forcing her gaze to meet mine. The vulnerability I saw there felt like a kick to my stomach because I knew how strong and resilient Stevie was. This situation had clearly rattled her.

"I'm so damn sorry," I said, my voice gruff with frustration. "I had no idea she was dropping Owen off early. I never would have knowingly put you in that position."

"I know it's not your fault, and it's fine. *I'm* fine," she lied, giving me a tremulous smile that didn't reach her eyes. "I should go…but my dress, bra, and shoes are still in the living room from last night."

Shit. More ammunition for Alyssa. "No, I want you to stay," I insisted, because the last thing I wanted was Stevie leaving with my ex's offensive remark swirling in her head and ruining our night together, which told me just how much I already cared about her. "Let me handle this situation with Alyssa first, and then we can talk. Please."

Her lips pursed, and I could see her internal debate, but much to my relief, she finally relented with a soft, "Okay."

Satisfied with that, I grabbed a T-shirt and shrugged it on, then stopped by Owen's bedroom and yeah, he was already on his Xbox, immersed in the world of Minecraft. He was still blissfully oblivious to the tension between adults, and for once I was grateful for the game's distraction.

I ruffled his hair to get his attention. "Hey, bud. I need you to wear your headphones for a while." The last thing I wanted was for him to hear what was undoubtedly going to be a heated conversation between his mother and me.

"Okay," he said, and without question he reached for the headset and covered up his ears.

I headed back out to the living room, where Alyssa had already made herself comfortable on the couch and was texting someone on her phone. It struck me, not for the first time, that for someone who was so outwardly beautiful, she was ugly on the inside. Selfish, mean, and manipulative. And bitter. She hadn't always been that way, but since the divorce those unattractive characteristics had magnified to the point that she was just toxic.

The fact that she could sit there so casually, as if she hadn't just belittled Stevie and called her a whore, made my blood pressure rise. "What the fuck, Alyssa?" I hissed furiously, not even knowing where to start when I had so many things to address. "What are you doing here? Owen has a drop-off time of two this afternoon, not *ten* this morning."

She set her phone aside and glanced at me, where I was standing on the other side of the coffee table that separated us. "He was whining and complaining and driving me nuts about getting home so he could play Minecraft."

And she'd clearly had ulterior motives and wanted to know if what Cece had told her about me bringing a woman up to my place last night was accurate. I had no doubts about that. "Regardless, you should have given me a heads-up that you were dropping him off early."

She smirked and arched a condescending brow. "And what, spoil the surprise?"

I jammed my hands on my hips, beyond enraged at her gall. "So, you admit that you did it deliberately."

Her shrug was pure arrogance. "I'll admit, I was curious to see if what Cece said was true."

My jaw clenched hard. "It's none of your fucking business what I do, and who I bring up to my place, when I don't have Owen." I stretched my hand out toward her. "Give me your key card to the penthouse."

She stiffened against the couch cushions, clearly not expecting that demand. "Why? You gave it to me so I'd have it in case of emergencies."

"Exactly." Which had never been a problem until now. "And considering you abused that power, and I'm not obligated to give you a key card to my place, I want it back. From now on, when you're bringing Owen home or picking him up, you can call or text me and I will allow Frank to send you up," I said of the doorman who vetted guests in the lobby. "Or I will meet you in the lobby. The choice will be mine, not yours."

Anger flashed in her eyes, but knowing I held the power in this situation, she dug into her purse and removed the key card from her wallet. Instead of handing it to me like any rational person would, she tossed it at my chest like a petulant child. Before I could grab it, the key card fell to the floor at my feet, and I picked it up, slipping it into my sweatpants' pocket.

Her gaze landed on the articles of clothing on the living room floor that wouldn't have been there had she arrived that afternoon at the designated time. "Jesus, when did you become so fucking tacky?" she asked, waving a hand at Stevie's discarded dress, bra, and shoes that made it very obvious what had transpired in front of the windows last night.

When did you become such a fucking bitch? Oh, wait, you've been that way for the past few years. I swallowed back the retort, refusing to engage with her.

I was right on the verge of telling her to leave when she asked, "So, who is the woman you brought home for the night?"

"None of your goddamn business."

"Oh, I think it is," she refuted.

"Jealousy doesn't look good on you, Lyss," I countered, knowing that was part of her issue.

She leaned back against the sofa, a devious look in her eyes. "I have every right to know who you're bringing around Owen. Surely you haven't forgotten that morality clause you insisted on adding to our divorce settlement?"

My stomach clenched. Of course I remembered. I'd been the one who'd demanded the morality clause based on *her* actions that led to our divorce. It had been my only way to try to regulate her behavior around Owen, which excluded allowing random men into her home and barring the use of alcohol and drugs when Owen was with her. It was ironic that she was now turning the tables on me, though I should have seen it coming.

"Those stipulations go both ways," she went on, glancing at her manicured nails as if she were discussing the weather and not issuing a threat. "If I remember correctly, it prohibits either of us from bringing around casual sex partners. You being in violation of the morality clause is not going to reflect well on you for the custody case. Hell, it might even cost you custody of Owen."

Her words made my blood run cold, because I had no doubt that she'd twist this situation to her advantage, regardless of the fact that she'd brought him home early. Not because she wanted custody of Owen, but hurting me was her goal and the only way to do that was through our son. She'd backed me into a corner and I only saw one way out. I had no choice and I'd deal with the repercussions of what I was about to do later. Right now, it was all about self-preservation and making sure my custody of Owen wasn't jeopardized in any way.

"Stevie isn't random or casual," I said, looking Alyssa dead in the eye and knowing that Stevie could likely hear this entire conversation. "She's a serious girlfriend and we're in a *committed* relationship. I am not in violation of the morality clause."

Alyssa's gaze narrowed skeptically. "Owen would have told me if you were seeing someone."

Why? Did she actually grill our son and try to pump Owen for information when she had him? *Of course she did.*

"*Because* of the morality clause, I was waiting to tell Owen about Stevie until I knew it was serious, and it is. And she isn't a stranger to Owen. He's met her many times in various public settings. He knows who she is."

"Where did you meet her?" Alyssa demanded to know. "Because clearly, she is not someone in our social circle. Trust me. No woman that I know would be caught dead wearing that cheap dress and those budget-friendly shoes."

"Yeah, well, some of us don't give a shit about those kinds of things," I said, which held true for me. Alyssa, on the other hand, had grown up surrounded by wealth and sadly, she measured a person's worth by those material possessions.

Alyssa stared me down. "Where did you meet her?" she asked again.

I knew she wouldn't hesitate to hire a PI to find out the answer to her question, and the last thing I wanted was anyone digging around in what I knew of Stevie's painful past and handing that information over to Alyssa to use as leverage. "I met her through Raven," I replied truthfully. "She works at The Back Door."

Alyssa gaped at me in shock, then she burst out laughing, the sound harsh and cruel. "Wait, she's a waitress? Isn't that a bit like slumming it for you? Or are you just thinking with your dick and not your head?"

My jaw clenched so hard I thought I'd break a molar. My protective instincts flared to life, and I glared at her, no compromise in my expression. "I'm only going to tell you this once, Alyssa. Unless you want to be slapped with a defamation of character suit, watch your mouth and what you say about Stevie. She's my girlfriend and a part of my life. She will also be in Owen's life and spending time with him, and I will not tolerate another inflammatory word against her, do you understand?" Considering the words that just came out of my mouth were unrehearsed and improvised, Stevie being my girlfriend sounded convincing even to my own ears.

Alyssa's lips pursed, her expression filled with spite after the way I'd just put her in her place for being disrespectful. She stood up, chin jutting out. "Sure, I'll watch what I say about her, but you'd better be careful, too. I'd really hate for you to lose custody of Owen if this ends up being a bunch of lies to cover your ass."

"Get out," I snapped, done with her bullshit. "I may have to deal with you because you're Owen's mother, but I do not have to put up with your condescending attitude in my home. Leave. *Now.*"

The corner of her mouth lifted in a sneer, but clearly realizing how pissed I was, she wisely didn't say anything more. She headed toward the elevator, not even bothering to say goodbye to Owen, as most mothers would considering she wouldn't see him for another week. But then again, as much as it pained me, I knew that Owen was nothing more than a pawn for her to use against me.

Once she was gone, I sank down into a chair, scrubbing my hands over my face and feeling emotionally drained. *Fuck*, now what was I going to do? The only thing I could, I realized, because I didn't have a choice.

I was going to make Stevie an offer she hopefully wouldn't be able to refuse.

CHAPTER SIX

Stevie

I'D NEVER BEEN one to eavesdrop, but it was difficult not to overhear the heated conversation between Caleb and Alyssa as it drifted down the hallway and into his bedroom. Their voices were raised, and there was no mistaking the anger in Caleb's tone, or the disdain in hers when it came to me.

I was normally a confident woman, but I couldn't deny the way she'd initially called me a whore, then mocked my clothing, my job, and insinuated that Caleb was *slumming it,* had dug up old insecurities. Because for a girl who'd grown up in a trailer park, a man like Caleb *was* out of my league. Not that he'd ever made me feel that way, but I could understand why anyone in his affluent social circle might look at me and wonder what a wealthy, gorgeous man like him was doing with a simple, unworldly woman like me.

There was also no misconstruing what he'd said to Alyssa. *Stevie isn't random or casual. She's a serious girlfriend and we're in a committed relationship.*

Yeah, that declaration made my jaw drop in shock.

Having been privy to their discussion, I understood why he'd tell Alyssa that lie. He had Owen to think about, and even though I doubted Caleb had violated that morality clause they'd talked about since Owen hadn't been here during our time together, he'd been nervous enough about the situation, and how Alyssa might twist it to make that statement.

And now, as I sat on his bed and listened to him order Alyssa to leave, I wondered how he was going to get himself out of that little lie.

A few minutes later, I heard him heading down the hall, then he walked into the bedroom carrying my dress, bra, and shoes. He looked harried and distressed, and I hated seeing him so troubled when he was a man who was always so composed and seemly unflappable.

"Is it safe to come out?" I joked, trying to lighten the moment.

A deep sigh escaped him as he set my clothing on the mattress beside me. "Yes, and I'm sorry you had to hear any of that." Genuine regret shimmered in his eyes.

My fingers absently pleated the hem of the T-shirt I was wearing. "You dug yourself a hole," I said with a teasing smile, because there was no ignoring what I'd overheard. "I'm not even close to being your serious girlfriend."

He grimaced and rubbed a hand along the back of his neck. "Yeah, about that…" He trailed off, obviously unsure of what he wanted to say or perhaps *how* he wanted to say it.

"Yes?"

"Can you and I discuss the possibility?"

"Of what?" I frowned, momentarily confused.

He held my gaze. "Of you being my girlfriend."

I blinked, stunned, his words the last thing I'd expected to hear.

"Temporarily," he was quick to add, as if he sensed I was about to reject that request. "Just until the custody case is over."

My head spun. Of all the ways I thought he might resolve the girlfriend comment he'd made to his ex-wife, asking for a pretend relationship for the next few months wasn't it.

"I…uh…" Still flustered by the request and certain his ex wouldn't buy the arrangement regardless, I shook my head and stared up at him. "Caleb…I don't think—"

"Dad, I'm hungry."

Interrupted by the smaller voice, my gaze went to the doorway of the bedroom to see Owen standing there the same time Caleb turned around. The tense set of his shoulders relaxed a fraction as he looked at his son.

"Didn't you have breakfast with your mom?" Caleb asked him.

Owen shook his head. "No. She woke me up and said she was bringing me home. I didn't have time to eat anything."

I couldn't see Caleb's face, which was probably

schooled for Owen's benefit, but I could easily imagine he was livid that Alyssa hadn't fed her own son because she'd been more concerned about getting to Caleb's to catch him in the act with a woman after being tipped off by a friend.

"I was just going to make some eggs," Caleb said in a neutral tone. "Want some?"

"No." Owen made a face that would have made me laugh under different circumstances. "Can I have cereal?"

"Sure," Caleb relented, clearly not in the mood for an argument with his boy.

Owen glanced around his father, and he smiled when he saw me sitting on the bed. "Hi, Stevie. What are you doing here?"

I wasn't sure how he'd missed seeing me earlier in the kitchen when he'd arrived, but I was grateful that he hadn't witnessed that awkward moment between myself and his dad. As to how to answer his question, I was at a loss for an explanation.

"I…um…"

Caleb jumped in. "Stevie came by to have breakfast with us."

Confusion creased between Owen's brows, but before he could ask any more questions Caleb strode over to Owen, turned him around, and ushered him out of the bedroom while looking over his shoulder at me. "We'll meet you out in the kitchen."

I nodded, and once they were gone, I took my dress and bra and went into the bathroom and changed so I wasn't walking around half naked. Finding a brush in a drawer, I restored some semblance of order to my hair, then exhaled a deep breath before joining them in the living area. Even though Owen had delayed our *girlfriend* conversation, I knew at some point we'd have to sort out the issue.

"Come sit by me, Stevie!" Owen said as soon as he saw me. He was already seated on a stool at the kitchen counter, digging into his Frosted Flakes and playing with two action figurines while Caleb was back at the stove, finishing the breakfast he'd started earlier.

I smiled at his enthusiasm. Because of Raven being Caleb's sister, I'd been around Owen enough the past year that we'd established a friendly and familiar rapport, so at least what Caleb told Alyssa about Owen knowing me was true.

"I'll be right there. I need a cup of coffee first," I told him, which was an understatement. I desperately needed a jolt of caffeine after this morning's fiasco, and to deal with the discussion with Caleb that still lay ahead.

I came up to the counter next to Caleb where the Keurig machine was located. He glanced my way as he continued scrambling eggs and reheating the mushrooms and ham.

"That coffee cup is for you," he said, nodding toward the navy blue mug he'd set out for me, along with creamer and sugar.

"Thank you." I put a pod into the machine and while I waited for my coffee to brew, I glanced at

Caleb. I was glad to see his earlier anger toward Alyssa had subsided, but he still looked unsettled.

"Are you okay?" I asked softly.

Despite everything, he managed a charming smile. "I will be if you agree to what I asked you earlier, before we were interrupted by Owen."

So many uncertainties about that request warred inside of me. "We'll talk…later, after we eat and Owen isn't listening in," I promised. I'd at least hear him out, despite my misgivings.

He divided up the eggs onto two plates, then added the warmed-up mushrooms and ham on top, along with a sprinkle of cheese. "I'm just taking it as a positive sign that you're still here."

I sighed, even as my stomach grumbled at the savory scent teasing my nose. "I haven't agreed to anything, Caleb."

His gaze held mine, and very seriously, he said, "I'm hoping you will."

The brewer finished the percolating process, and while I added sugar and creamer to the coffee, Caleb carried our plates to the kitchen island. He set one next to Owen, and instead of sitting beside his son, he indicated that I should take that spot while he stood across the counter so he was facing us.

"So what fun things did you do with your mom this week?" Caleb asked his son after we ate a few bites of the eggs.

"Nothing." Owen set down the Iron Man figurine he'd been playing with and took another bite of his cereal. Milk dripped down his chin and he wiped it away with the back of his hand. "I went to school, and I stayed with Grandma and Grandpa because Mommy wasn't feeling well."

I didn't miss the way Caleb's body tensed. "What do you mean Mommy wasn't feeling well?" he asked, his tone far more casual than his posture. "Was it like last time?"

"Yeah. She had a headache and was sleeping a lot. She called Grandma who came and got me."

Caleb's gaze flickered to mine, and the worry I saw there was concerning. The fact that this seemed to be a regular occurrence didn't bode well.

"Stevie, look at this," Owen said, abruptly jumping to a more interesting topic as only a six-year-old could as he turned toward me with a Spider-Man action figure in his hand. "Look at what Spidey can do!"

He lifted the toy's arm and aimed it at me, then pressed a button and out shot a small white net that landed on my shoulder. I gasped dramatically, and Owen chortled, making me grin at his unfettered glee, which was exactly what I needed after this morning's debacle. Even Caleb chuckled at his son's tickled reaction.

"I gotcha with his web!" Owen said, then removed the little projectile from my dress. "Want to see what my other action heroes can do?"

"Not now, Owen," Caleb said, redirecting his son's attention. "How about you finish up your cereal. When you're done, you can play Minecraft for a little longer, with the headphones on, while I talk to Stevie about grown-up stuff."

At the mention of more video game time, he quickly finished his Frosted Flakes. He nearly leapt off the stool to run to his room but Caleb stopped him before he could.

"Hey, you know the rules," Caleb said in a gentle, but firm tone. "Clear your dishes and rinse them, please."

Owen did as he was told without complaint, then grabbed his toys and disappeared into his room.

Caleb shook his head after he was gone. "I usually regulate the time he spends on his Xbox, but it's coming in handy today."

We finished our own breakfast, which was delicious. I helped Caleb clean the kitchen, putting the dishes into the dishwasher while he wiped down the counters and stovetop. The easy silence between us felt normal, but knowing the discussion still to come, anticipation churned in my stomach.

"Let's go sit in the living room where it's comfortable," he suggested, his tone gentle but carrying an underlying seriousness. "This conversation might take a while because you need to know why it's so important to me that you say yes to what I'm going to propose."

I followed him into the adjoining room and sat down on the sofa, and he settled into the club chair next to me. I folded my hands in my lap, a nervous energy sliding through me.

He leaned forward, bracing his elbows on his knees as his gaze met mine, showing me a surprising glimpse of vulnerability for a man who was usually so confident and composed. "Clearly, you heard the conversation with Alyssa, which gives you a good indication of where things stand between us."

"Yes," I said with a nod. "And I hope it's okay, but Raven did mention that things are contentious between the two of you, but I had no idea she was so…"

"Vindictive? Spiteful? Resentful to the point of wanting me to suffer emotionally?" He laughed, though the sound lacked any humor. "Yeah, they all apply."

I heard the pain in his voice, and my heart hurt for him. "Was she always that way?" I asked curiously, unable to imagine Caleb marrying a woman so callous and cruel, yet he had.

"Maybe? I don't know." He shook his head at his own confusion. "The thing is, I never would have dated her had she shown me that side to her personality, but she did change after we got married, so that's where my 'maybe' comes in. Because maybe those tendencies were always there, but she did a great job of concealing them until things in our marriage started to change and deteriorate."

"Then you loved her at some point," I said, the words tumbling out before I could stop them.

He sighed, the sound full of regret. "I cared for her, yes. I can't say I was ever madly in love with her." He paused for a beat, his eyes flicking to the floor, then back to mine. "My mother set us up. Alyssa is the daughter of one of her affluent friends, so they pushed us together, because that's how my mother is. Everything is about status and appearance for her. So, when Alyssa got pregnant with Owen, I stupidly felt pressured to marry her even though I knew in my gut that it didn't feel right. But a part of me did like the idea of having a wife and a family, so I went into it with good intentions."

Of course he had. Caleb struck me as a man who was honorable and upstanding. One who believed in doing things for the right reasons, even at the cost of his own happiness. I couldn't help but feel for him, even though I didn't fully understand the pressure he must have been under.

"So what happened?" I asked, my voice softer now, intrigued by the story he was revealing.

"After Owen was born, things changed. Alyssa changed." He stared down at his clasped hands, avoiding my gaze for a moment, as if he was still working through the memories. "There'd always been a disconnect between us, but things got progressively worse. I'd just become partner at Manhattan Prestige Realty and I was spending a lot of time at the office, which she didn't like. She wanted the money and status of being my wife, but she didn't like the time I dedicated to work and we fought about that a lot, even though I did my best to juggle work with home life and spending time with Owen."

He rubbed a hand along the back of his neck, and

I could see the shadows of that tumultuous past on his face. "But no matter what I did, it was never enough for her and quite frankly, dealing with her mood swings and the tension she created in our relationship became exhausting. To put things into context, she's an only child, entitled, used to getting her way, and having all the attention on her. When I didn't bend to her demands her resentment toward me grew."

I could sense the frustration building in him, and I remained quiet, giving him the space to continue.

"That's when I really saw her malicious side, and everything she did after that was all in an attempt to hurt me because she felt wronged. First, it was racking up an obscene amount in credit card debt like a spoiled child. She started ignoring Owen and leaving him with a sitter so she could go out during the day without him, and even at night. She told me she needed a life and that she wanted to spend time with her girlfriends after being cooped up with Owen all day...except I discovered she was out having affairs with random men."

I winced, unable to imagine how awful that realization must have been for him. "I'm so sorry." I didn't know what else to say...but I did find it ironic that Alyssa could be so judgmental toward me when her own choices and past actions were so questionable.

He shrugged, but I could tell this entire conversation, and revisiting the past, weighed heavily on him. "A part of me felt like maybe I drove her to that, but when I found out she was abusing prescription drugs on top of everything else, that was a deal breaker for me. Clearly, she was miserable, and so was I. And, mostly, there was no way I could trust her around Owen." His voice cracked with pain. "I filed for divorce, and the only way she was allowed joint custody was if she checked herself into rehab, which her parents pushed her into. She was there for four months and she honestly thought I'd take her back once she was clean, but I was done with her, which is the impetus for her bitterness and resentment and fighting me for sole custody of Owen. For one thing it would give her more money in child support on top of alimony, but she also knows how much losing Owen would destroy me."

"But you're a great dad." My brow furrowed in confusion as I stared at him. "How could that even happen?"

His lips stretched into a grim line, but his eyes were full of frustration and helplessness. "Here's the kicker. Alyssa's father is a judge with connections in family court here in New York. And despite everything, he has blinders on when it comes to his daughter. She's a daddy's girl and he would do anything to make her happy. And that morality clause? I'm the one who insisted on it when we divorced because of her history of random affairs and drug use, but I don't want to give her any ammunition to use against me, which brings us back around to me asking you to stand in as my girlfriend for the next two months."

CARLY PHILLIPS & ERIKA WILDE

His eyes bore into mine, so expectant and hopeful, while my own heartbeat quickened in my chest. "Standing in as your girlfriend...what does that even entail?"

"Accompanying me to business dinners, and an upcoming art charity gala that I know Alyssa will be attending. Being seen with me in public and spending time with me and Owen, and making sure the doorman sees you around. Just being a part of our lives for the next two months so it's clear to anyone who might be watching that we're a legitimate couple."

His choice of words caught my attention. "Anyone who might be watching?"

He hesitated for a moment, then very reluctantly said, "I'm pretty sure that Alyssa is going to hire a PI to find out what's going on between you and me. And that's why I need everything to look real."

My head started to pound, and I rubbed at my temples with my fingers, trying to process, well, everything.

He reached out and grabbed my free hand, and when I raised my eyes to his, I didn't miss the imploring look on his handsome face. "I know this is an incredibly selfish request, but I can't risk losing Owen. Please."

I had a difficult time trying to wrap my mind around everything he was asking of me. "Caleb, I have my own life. I work nights and most weekends at The Back Door. I work as an intern at Dare PR twice a week and I have a degree I'm trying to finish—"

"I'll make it worth your while," he interrupted, and now there was an edge of desperation to his voice. "I won't interfere with your internship, or your studies, but I would need you to take a leave from The Back Door because I'll need you around in the evenings and on the weekends."

I jumped up from my spot on the couch, my mind whirling. "I can't—"

"You can because Raven will understand," he argued, standing too. "Especially when you tell her the reason why. I know I'm asking a lot, but I'm prepared to offer you fifty thousand dollars for two months, just until the custody case is over."

The amount was so staggering, so unexpected, that my jaw literally dropped. "What?" I asked, certain I must have misheard him.

"Think of it as a business deal. A temporary job. Two months of your time for fifty grand."

Fifty grand...Part of me was insulted he was trying to buy my help, but I knew he was desperate. I thought about all the things I could do with a lump sum of money like that. Pay off most of my school loans. Get an apartment in a nicer neighborhood. Help out Valerie until she was settled again. Actually put some of it away into savings. Fifty grand was nothing to a man like Caleb...and life-changing for me.

And all I would have to do was pretend to be his girlfriend for two months.

Not really a hardship, except for the fact that a part of me wished it were for real. Because the truth was, I might have only spent one night with him, but this crush I'd had on him for the past year already felt like it was blossoming into something more. But he wasn't asking for a true commitment, and after everything he'd been through with Alyssa I could easily understand why he'd have his emotional guard up.

"Please," he said softly.

He looked genuinely terrified of losing custody of Owen, and compared to that pain, he was asking for two months out of my life. I could do this for Caleb, because I'd never be able to forgive myself if he lost his son over something I could have prevented from happening.

I swallowed hard. Somehow I knew this situation had the potential of leaving my heart in tatters, but this wasn't about me, but Owen's welfare because the little boy would be equally traumatized without his father in his life.

"Okay, I'll do it," I said, and hoped I didn't come to regret my decision.

CHAPTER SEVEN

Caleb

PROFOUND RELIEF SURGED through me the moment Stevie agreed to stand in as my girlfriend, even though prior to Alyssa's impromptu arrival I'd been thinking of dating her. We'd leapt right over that slow and steady exploration of our attraction and headlong into an exclusive, committed *fake* relationship for appearances' sake.

It was enough to make *my* head spin, and I knew by Stevie's wary agreement she was completely overwhelmed by everything that had happened. Even now, as I drove her to her apartment after leaving Owen with my sister, Cara, watching over him for the next hour, her uncertainty was nearly tangible. She'd been incredibly quiet during the drive, staring out the passenger window of my Audi R8 as I followed the directions she'd given me to her place in Elmhurst, Queens.

A part of me felt guilty for coercing Stevie into this mess that was currently my life, but my options were limited and I wasn't taking any chances with Owen's well-being. There was no doubt in my mind that I'd be dealing with Alyssa's scrutiny over the next two months, that she'd try to find any way to tarnish my reputation and she wouldn't have hesitated to drag Stevie into the fray, too.

The truth was, if I hadn't claimed Stevie as my girlfriend, Alyssa would have painted a very sordid picture for her attorney of what she'd walked in on. She wouldn't think twice about maligning Stevie's character in the worst ways in order to further her own agenda, and the only way to protect Stevie from my ex's malicious motives was to make her a part of my life.

Right now, with the custody case looming over me, Stevie being my serious girlfriend gave *us* more credibility than if she'd just been a one-night stand.

I know what I was asking of her was a lot—I'd seen her reluctance to get involved—but I had every intention of making it worth her while and judging by her reaction to the fifty grand I intended to pay her, I'd accomplished that goal. I got the impression she didn't have much, and if that money eased her finances a bit in exchange for her being a part of mine and Owen's life for the next couple months, then it was a win-win situation in my opinion.

Because Stevie had been so hesitant to accept my proposal, I'd told her to think of our agreement as a business deal, a temporary job, and I definitely regretted phrasing our situation that way when my attraction to Stevie was far more than just a fleeting proposition.

As much as this fake relationship between us was for show, I truly liked the idea of spending more time with her, and now I had the chance to do so legitimately.

The circumstances weren't ideal, and as stressful as the predicament was with Alyssa, I wasn't mad about Stevie being a more integrated part of my life. In fact, shockingly, I welcomed it. She was the only woman since my divorce that had captured my attention so thoroughly and made me want to open myself up to the possibilities of…something more with someone again. And if this situation gave me the opportunity to explore that option with Stevie, then I was willing to take the risk, no matter how complicated it might get.

"Does your sister live close by?" Stevie asked, breaking the silence between us and surprising me with her random question. "She was at your place less than ten minutes after you'd called her to watch Owen."

I smiled when I remembered Cara's startled reaction to finding Stevie at my apartment when she'd arrived earlier. And her surprise when I told her that I was seeing Stevie exclusively. I didn't explain the situation to Cara. I felt it was best, and easiest, to let her believe we were really a couple. There were a few people who were going to have to be privy to the truth—Stevie's sister, Valerie, Raven, and even my partner at work, Beck Daniels—but the less who knew we were perpetuating a lie, the better.

I continued to follow the directions to Stevie's place via the car's navigation system, glad to have her talking again about something other than Alyssa, or our arrangement. "She actually lives in the building in one of the apartments I own."

"*One* of the apartments you own?" she asked incredulously.

I shrugged, keeping my eyes on the road. "I'm a realtor. I sell *and* buy properties for investment purposes. I own six other apartments other than my own at The Cortland and lease them out," I explained. "After everything that happened between Lance and Raven last year, and my mother siding with my brother during his trial when he'd clearly assaulted Raven, Cara wanted out from under my mother's thumb. She's so much younger than Raven and me, but she's a good kid, and the only way Cara could move out was if I helped her, since my mother refused to support her in any way."

The muscles across my shoulders tightened as I spoke, because every time I thought about my mother's refusal to assist Cara, it made me furious. I knew I was doing the right thing by providing a place for her to live, but it didn't erase the sting of how my mother selectively treated me, Raven, and Cara, while putting Lance on a pedestal. Despite him being in prison. It was such a fucked-up situation.

"You're a good brother," Stevie said, her voice breaking through my thoughts, soft and sincere. "To both Raven and Cara."

"I try to be," I said as I drove the car over the Queensboro Bridge.

Stevie rested her head against the back of the leather seat and smiled at me. "Raven mentioned Cara is attending the Fashion Institute of Technology."

"She is, which makes living at The Cortland convenient since the institute is only ten minutes away. That, and I like being able to keep an eye on her." I switched lanes to maneuver around a slower vehicle. "And having her close by is nice because, like today, I can call her up and have her watch Owen when I can't get my regular sitter at the last minute. She adores Owen, and he loves her too."

"It's nice that she's taking him out to the waterfront and for an ice cream," Stevie said, glancing back out the window with a sigh. "It's a beautiful day."

I agreed. "I'll probably meet up with them after I drop you off."

Even as I said the words, I wished she were coming along and spending the afternoon with us. I thought about asking, but considering what I'd already roped Stevie into, I didn't want to press my luck. Besides, she undoubtedly needed time to decompress after this morning's ambush with Alyssa.

"I do have a question for you," she said when another comfortable stretch of silence passed between us. "I saw the concerned look on your face this morning when Owen told you about Alyssa not feeling well this past week and him staying with her parents. Do you worry about her relapsing?"

"I'd be lying if I didn't say the thought wasn't in the back of my mind. But I do know she's prone to getting migraines, or so she says, so I can't jump to those conclusions. Not without evidence," I said, even though it was difficult *not* to make those assumptions. "But yes…it's concerning because I'm not sure how closely her parents regulate her. They had a difficult time facing the truth that she had an addiction problem to begin with, and they think she's fine just because she went to rehab and completed the treatment program, but there's always the chance of her falling back into addiction."

The navigation had me turning down a street that made me frown. For the most part, Elmhurst, Queens, wasn't a bad place to live. As a realtor, I knew it was solidly middle class with some decent gentrified areas, but it was the outer lying areas of the community where we currently were that I found questionable and concerning.

"That's my place, right there," she pointed out. "You can drop me off at the curb."

My gut twisted with unease as I slowed the car as we approached an older brick apartment building and I slid into a vacant spot between two beat-up, unkempt cars. The exterior of where Stevie lived wasn't well maintained, nor was the general neighborhood. The area was run-down, the buildings and homes neglected and weathered.

As soon as I parked, she started to open her door to get out. "Thank you for the ride—"

I caught her wrist to stop her before she could take off, and she glanced at me in surprise.

"I'm not just *dropping you off*," I insisted, my tone as stern as my stare. "I'll walk you to your apartment."

She had the audacity to roll her eyes at me. "For crying out loud, Caleb, I've lived here for three years. I know it's not the greatest neighborhood, but it's broad daylight and I'll be fine. It's better than when I arrive home after a night shift at the bar, but that's why I carry pepper spray."

My jaw clenched. Her alone and vulnerable at night wasn't something I wanted to consider. "There isn't even a security door leading into the complex to keep anyone out," I said, then scowled, my defenses flaring as I watched a group of twenty-something-year-old men walk out from the park next to her complex, a breeding ground for crime and drug deals.

"I'm walking you to your door," I all but growled.

She arched a brow, giving me a bit of attitude. "Are you sure you want to leave your fancy sports car parked out here, unattended?"

She had a point. My Audi stuck out like a sore thumb, along with a black BMW parked a few car lengths ahead of us. And those guys who'd just exited the park were eyeing the R8 like it was theirs for the taking, but I didn't give a shit. Stevie's welfare was far more important. A car was replaceable. Stevie was not.

"I'll take my chances," I said, meaning it as I released her wrist. "That's what insurance is for."

"Fine."

She huffed out an annoyed sigh I would have found amusing if I wasn't so on edge about where she lived. Which on some level I recognized as ridiculous considering she'd resided here for three years, without incident. It didn't matter. One night with Stevie and my protective instincts toward her were on overdrive.

We got out of the car and I met up with her on the cracked and uneven sidewalk. We started toward the brick building, with me glaring at the men who were eyeing Stevie in her sexy dress and heels from last night, despite me being with her. Oblivious to those leers, she absently glanced over at the black BMW parked at the curb up ahead and abruptly stopped walking, her posture stiff and her expression startled. She must not have seen the car when we'd driven up, because she was now staring at it with a look of trepidation.

I stopped beside Stevie, her troubled reaction confusing me. "Is everything okay?"

Before she could answer, the vehicle flipped a quick U-turn and sped away in the opposite direction.

She glanced at me, her unease palpable. "I'm pretty sure that was Mark's car."

"Mark?" I asked, trying to follow her explanation.

"Valerie's ex," she said, reminding me of the conversation we'd had last night at the party, of the abusive relationship her sister had just gotten out of.

"Are you sure?"

She nodded. "Ninety-nine percent. He drives a black BMW, and just like your car, there aren't a lot of sports cars like that around here," she said, and then her eyes flared with fear. "Shit, if that was Mark I need to check on my sister and make sure she's okay."

She turned toward the apartment building and all but ran up the sidewalk leading to the entrance. My long strides kept me by her side.

"I thought you said there was a restraining order against him," I said, as we entered the complex. There was no lobby, no security or safeguards in place whatsoever to protect the residents, and definitely no amenities. Just a bank of metal mailboxes, an elevator with an "out of order" sign posted on the doors, and a flight of stairs straight ahead.

She scoffed as she rushed up the first set of steps. "Like that would keep an egomaniac like Mark away from Valerie."

I couldn't argue with her logic which was fueling her anxiety, and since I had no idea where her apartment was, I could only follow her up two flights of stairs to a third story. Out of breath, she dug through her purse as we hurried down a hallway, and when she reached her place she used a key to unlock the door.

She burst inside, leaving the door open for me to come in, too. "Valerie!" she yelled in a panic when an initial sweep of the very miniscule living room and kitchenette showed no signs of her sister.

"Jesus, Stevie, I'm right in here sorting clothes for the laundromat," Valerie said, walking out of what I assumed was a bedroom, carrying a basket with clothes. "You don't have to shout."

A startled look passed over Valerie's features at seeing me there, too. "Oh, hey...hi, Caleb—"

"Was Mark here?" Stevie demanded to know, interrupting any pleasantries.

Confusion flickered in Valerie's eyes. "What are you talking about?"

"I'm pretty sure I saw his car parked outside the building."

Valerie set the laundry basket down on the couch, her demeanor turning cautious. "You *think*, or you for sure saw him?"

"It was a black BMW, Val," Stevie said, and I could hear the genuine worry in her voice. "I don't know if Mark was for sure behind the wheel, but what are the chances of a car like his being in this neighborhood, just hanging out in front of the apartment building?"

Valerie visibly paled, which told me how frightened of this asshole she was. "If he was here, he didn't come up to the apartment."

Stevie's lips flattened into a grim line. "Maybe he didn't have the chance to because he saw me first."

Finally, I stepped forward and offered my advice. "You should call the police and report the incident."

"There's no proof," Valerie said, shaking her head, which did nothing to chase away the distress that was plain on her face. "The restraining order does prohibit Mark from contacting me in any way. By phone, text, email, social media, or in person, but…if he didn't actually come up to the apartment, neither I nor Stevie can prove that he was here because it would be his word against mine."

That was true because there were *no fucking security cameras* to record and catch suspicious activities around the building. I was beyond frustrated by those lack of safety measures, but kept my tone neutral. "If you report it, the police will at least have it on record."

"He's right, Val," Stevie said, taking her sister's hands in hers and looking into her eyes. "If Mark is getting ballsy enough to start stalking you again, then we need to make sure these incidents are reported because there's no telling what lines he's capable of crossing."

Valerie folded her arms over her chest, as if trying to hold herself together. She nodded her agreement, tears of legitimate fear shimmering in her eyes, which gave me a good indication of how scared she was of this asshole. That despite a restraining order, she knew her safety was in jeopardy. And by association, Stevie was equally vulnerable if Valerie's ex was that determined to get to her, by any means necessary.

The whole situation set me on edge and I had to take a deep, calming breath while Stevie consoled her sister, then retrieved her cellphone from her purse and made a call to the police to file the report for Valerie, which she was able to do over the phone.

That gave me too much time to look around the apartment, to really realize how small the place was with minimal furnishings, though the living area was neat and tidy, and so was the compact kitchenette. From what I could see, there was only one bedroom. The fact that there was a blanket and pillow folded up on the couch told me that Valerie was probably sleeping on the sofa for now.

I regarded the less-than-desirable neighborhood. Both of the women's safety. The cramped apartment. I took everything into consideration and came to a single conclusion which I expressed to Stevie once she was off the phone.

"Okay, that's done," she said, setting her cellphone aside before glancing back at me. "Thank you for bringing me home, and I appreciate your concern, but we'll be fine—"

"You're not living here," I interrupted her, my tone unapologetically direct. "You're moving into one of my apartments at The Cortland."

She gaped at me, then quickly bristled, spine straightening. "I might have agreed to be your pretend girlfriend, but that doesn't give you the right to dictate where I'm going to live."

I was getting a quick lesson on just how independent and stubborn Stevie was. Which, admittedly, impressed *and* aroused me because it tapped into a very alpha, dominant side of my personality that had the urge to show her who the boss really was in this situation.

"Pretend girlfriend?" Valerie glanced between the two of us in confusion.

"A lot has happened since last night," Stevie told her sister. "I'll explain later."

"Ohhkay," Valerie said, looking intrigued by this new dynamic between me and Stevie as she took a step back. "I think I'm just going to go hang out in the bedroom and let the two of you hash out your living arrangements."

Stevie's lips pursed. "There are no living arrangements to hash out."

Valerie glanced at me, and seeing my determined stance, a small smile touched the corner of her lips before she shifted her gaze back to her sister. "You know, I'm betting on Caleb winning this argument, but give it your best shot, Stevie."

Valerie turned around and walked into the adjoining bedroom with Stevie glaring after her for siding with me. I had the urge to laugh, but Stevie was not amused and I was already bracing for a battle and didn't need to aggravate her any more than she already was.

I didn't mean to bulldoze her. But after what I'd seen, compromising on this issue wasn't an option for me. My offer would at least give her two months to figure out a different place to live, and with the money I planned to transfer into her bank account in the morning, she'd definitely be able to afford an upgraded apartment with security for her and Valerie once her commitment to me was through and she was ready to move on.

She lifted her chin. "Thank you for the offer, but I'm not taking advantage of your generosity. You're already paying me a small fortune to be your girlfriend. Living at The Cortland is above and beyond what we discussed or agreed upon."

No, she didn't strike me as a woman who'd ever take advantage of me or my money, which only made her that much more attractive to me. That authenticity also made me want to give her all those luxuries she'd clearly grown up without, because I knew she'd appreciate them without entitlement.

"It is more than we discussed," I agreed as I slowly closed the distance between us, which didn't take long in the tiny living room. "And you're not taking advantage of anything because I'm insisting on making this a nonnegotiable part of the deal we made."

She tipped her head back to look up at me and arched a brow. "Nonnegotiable?" she repeated, her tone incredulous.

"Yes. As in, not up for argument." I gentled my tone. "I have a fully furnished, currently unleased apartment and it's yours for two months, or longer if you need it. And since I'm insisting on you staying at The Cortland, I'll pay the rent on this apartment for the next two months so you don't lose it, and you can decide what you want to do once the custody case with Owen is over."

Her chin jutted out. "I'm not leaving Valerie."

"That's not an issue," I assured her. "She's coming with you. The apartment has two bedrooms. There's plenty of room for both of you, and as I said, it's fully furnished. And most importantly, the building is secure, with a doorman and security cameras, and she'll be safer there than here."

She opened her mouth to say something, but before she could issue any other argument, I quickly continued.

"This place is not safe, and neither is this neighborhood, Stevie," I reiterated. "And being my girlfriend, there is no fucking way I'd let you live here." Hell, even *not* being my legitimate girlfriend I was having a difficult time with her living in this neighborhood.

"An apartment in your building wasn't part of the deal," she said, and I didn't miss the flicker of pride in her eyes.

"I'm making it part of the deal," I said softly. "It's a matter of safety. If I ever need you to pick up Owen, or be with him...this area would not go over well with Alyssa."

Finally, Stevie nodded in understanding. "Okay."

Relieved, I reached out and slid my hand along her neck and beneath the fall of her hair, grateful when she didn't pull away but instead leaned into my touch. I skimmed my thumb along her jawline as she looked up at me. "Thank you."

"I'm starting to feel like a kept woman," she grumbled beneath her breath.

Grinning, I resisted the urge to tell her to get used to it, that I was already starting to enjoy spoiling her. Instead, I said, "I would *never* mistake you for being a kept woman. You're much too stubborn and self-sufficient for that."

Her full lips finally curved with a smile, the first one since before Alyssa had barged into my apartment and changed the course of my relationship with Stevie. For the better, I was hoping, though I sensed it was going to take more to convince her that my growing feelings for her weren't for the sake of pretenses.

Without even thinking because it felt so natural, I tipped her head back and touched my mouth to hers. The contact started off soft and slow, and she even sighed against my lips as her hands came up and pressed lightly against my chest. But then the kiss gradually deepened, real and potent, and she didn't hold back as our lips parted and I swept my tongue inside, swirling and tangling with hers, quickly elevating the desire smoldering between us. My dick hardened, and forcibly reminding myself that Valerie was right in the next room, I finally let us both back up for air before I pushed her down on the couch and did all the dirty, wicked things to her playing through my mind.

Stevie stared up at me, her eyes soft, all of her obstinance gone. Mostly, anyway.

"Two months," she said breathlessly. "That's it."

"Agreed," I replied with a triumphant grin, taking it as a win. "And you're moving in today, so pack whatever you and Valerie need to get through the next few days, and we'll come back for the rest later."

That glimpse of a teasing sparkle in her eye, along with a sassy salute and an equally impudent "Yes, sir" told me we'd weathered the storm. That things were mostly back to normal between us and would hopefully stay that way.

CHAPTER EIGHT

Stevie

"IF THIS IS a dream, I don't ever want to wake up."

Valerie sighed in awe as she drank her Monday morning cup of coffee and stared out the floor-to-ceiling windows overlooking the Hudson River. I understood her amazement because I was still trying to wrap my own mind around the fact that my sister and I were living at The Cortland, in a luxurious and spacious two-bedroom residence with the kind of comforts and amenities far beyond our budgets. I was starting to feel as though I was living in a *Pretty Woman* movie.

"No, it's not a dream, but it's not our reality, either," I reminded my sister as I joined her in the living room with my own mug of coffee, silently agreeing that our multi-million-dollar view was spectacular—and yes, I'd googled the cost of one of these apartments and nearly had a heart attack. "This arrangement with Caleb is temporary, as you know."

Valerie glanced at me with a smile, looking more relaxed and, dare I say, happy than I'd seen her since her split with Mark. "Yes, I know, but damn, let me enjoy every single second of living like the other one percent."

I laughed, unable to begrudge her that.

Last night, after Caleb got us settled into our new apartment and ordered us more groceries than I'd ever had at one time delivered to stock the cupboards and refrigerator, I'd sat down with Valerie and told her everything. From how Alyssa had deliberately arrived early to drop off Owen, to how I now held the title of Caleb's girlfriend.

She'd found the whole arrangement amusing, while I was still finding it difficult to process how in just twenty-four hours my life had completely changed into one I didn't recognize. It wasn't easy accepting all this from Caleb, even for a short time, but I understood why it was important—for the sake of appearances and so Alyssa didn't have any leverage to use over Caleb for the custody case. And for Valerie's safety, too, for which I was grateful, because there was no way of Mark knowing where Valerie was living now, since we hadn't left a forwarding address.

As much as I'd initially fought Caleb's offer to move us into The Cortland because I wasn't one to take handouts, I was relieved, mostly for my sister's sake. I told myself living in this apartment for two months wasn't charity. It was part of the deal I'd made with Caleb and as long as I remembered that, I'd be fine.

A knock on the door surprised us both. Even

though it was mid-morning, I knew it could only be one of two people—Caleb or Cara since they both lived in the building—and I hadn't yet had a chance to put anyone on my "approved" list of guests with the doorman.

I headed into the foyer and looked through the peephole. Seeing Caleb standing on the other side, I opened the door.

"Hi," I said breathlessly, feeling a little hot and bothered at how gorgeous he looked in his work suit. Dark gray and fitting his body to tailored perfection, staring at him was equivalent to a woman's version of looking at porn because that whole executive, big dick energy radiating from him was arousing as hell.

He grinned, looking genuinely happy to see me. "I brought fresh, hot donuts, which I picked up after dropping Owen off at school," he said, lifting a box imprinted with a name of some fancy shop in the area. "I thought you two might enjoy them with your morning coffee."

"Oh, my God, come in already," Valerie called out from behind me. "You had me at fresh, hot donuts."

I rolled my eyes at my sister's enthusiasm, but I was smiling as I stepped aside to give Caleb room to enter. He walked past me, and a whiff of his expensive cologne had me weak in the knees because like Pavlov's dog, the arousing scent immediately took me back to Saturday night, and sex with him.

Stifling a groan, I followed him into the kitchen where he put the box on the counter. Valerie didn't waste any time diving in and selecting a chocolate cruller for herself.

"Thank you for the donuts, and not to sound ungrateful, but what are you doing here?" I asked him. It was a Monday morning. I'd expected him to be at the office.

He shrugged. "I wanted to check in with you two, see how last night was, and how you're settling in."

"I slept like a baby after a bath in that deep soaking tub in my bathroom," Valerie chimed in before I could answer. "It's so quiet here and my bed is like sleeping on a soft cloud."

Caleb chuckled. "I'm glad you slept well," he said, then shifted his gaze to me for an answer.

"Same," I replied, agreeing with my sister. Without any outside noise, no weird sounds from the park next to our complex, or neighbor dogs barking interrupting my sleep, I'd crashed hard last night. "I'm very well rested, thank you."

"Good. I also wanted to let you know that your key card gives you access to all the building's amenities, so feel free to take advantage of the pool and sauna and yoga studio. And there's also a rooftop terrace you can enjoy, as well." He slid his hands into the front pockets of his slacks. "So, what are you two up to today?" he asked, changing the subject.

"Finishing unpacking," Valerie said, more chatty than I'd seen her in weeks. "And I'm submitting my résumé to Dare PR, so fingers crossed that works out."

"Good luck," Caleb said with a grin, then glanced at me again. "And what about you?"

I leaned my hip against the counter. "I need to finish writing a paper for one of my classes, along with studying for an upcoming test I have in macroeconomics. And I have a shift tonight at The Back Door."

That easygoing smile on his face faded a bit. "Are you going to take a leave like we discussed?"

"Yes, but I need to talk to Raven," I told him. "I'm not just leaving her shorthanded, so it might take a week or two until she can fully cover my shifts."

I saw his jaw tighten and his eye twitch, and raised a brow at him. "Why do you look like you're going to have an aneurysm?"

Valerie snickered, clearly seeing the shift in Caleb's mood, too.

"I don't," he insisted.

"Yes, you do," I argued, pretty sure I knew the cause of his displeasure.

"Yeah, this is my cue to leave and go finish unpacking my things," Valerie said, sounding amused. She grabbed another donut and disappeared down the hallway and into one of the bedrooms.

Once she was gone, I crossed my arms over my chest and returned my attention back to Caleb—a man clearly used to getting his way—and who still wore a disgruntled expression. "Why are you looking at me like that?"

"Like what?" he replied, his tone gruff.

"With that furrow between your brows like you're

not happy about something, and that little vein popping out near your temple is a dead giveaway, too." That I could read him so well already was shocking.

His stiff shoulders relaxed, and the look on his face turned to concern. "I would just feel better if you didn't have to work at The Back Door in the evenings."

I'd never had a man be so protective over me, and as much as I appreciated the gesture—and even secretly liked it—I wasn't some delicate, weak female who needed to depend on a man, for anything. "Raven works there in the evenings," I pointed out.

"And so does Remy," he shot back, jamming his hands on his hips. "He's there to take her home every night and make sure she gets there safely."

"Oh, my God," I said incredulously, and tossed my hands up in the air in frustration. "You're being a caveman, Caleb."

The man had the nerve to smirk, his entire demeanor shifting as he braced his hands on either side of my hips against the counter and leaned in close. "How about you come up to my place with me right now and I'll show you just how much of a caveman I can be?"

Feeling the light press of his body against mine, a tantalizing tease, I shivered, my nipples tightening and heat settling low in my belly. It was crazy to me how he could flip my own annoyance into arousal so easily.

Trying to distract myself, I reached over to the donut box and took a powdered, pillowy one that looked like it was filled with something. "Don't you have to go to work?" I asked, and took a small bite of the donut, the powdered sugar sprinkling everywhere—my lips, my chin, and probably the front of my T-shirt, too.

"I'm a partner," he murmured, his gaze falling to my mouth as though he was imagining licking away the confectioner's sugar. "My hours are flexible. I can take *hours* off if I want to."

His insinuation was clear and God he was so damned tempting. I wasn't going to pretend that I didn't want him. That there wouldn't be sex between us during our two-month situationship because I knew resisting him was going to be impossible. But I wasn't about to crumble and follow him up to his apartment right on the heels of him trying to make some kind of point.

I was making a point, too, and I wouldn't be swayed by amazing sex or the promise of orgasms.

So, instead, I bit deeper into the donut, purposefully making the Bavarian cream ooze out near the corner of my mouth. A groan rumbled in his chest as I slowly, seductively, licked the dollop of cream away in a very suggestive manner, distracting him from the ridiculous conversation, and also feeling his dick hardening against me.

"Go to work, Caleb," I said huskily. *Before I take you up on your offer.* "I have schoolwork to get done."

He reluctantly pushed away and straightened, desire still darkening his eyes. "Fine, but we'll talk later."

I had no doubt that we would.

CHAPTER NINE

Stevie

I SPENT THE rest of the morning and early afternoon writing a paper for my business communication class and also studying for my upcoming macroeconomics test. I wasn't one of those students that retained information easily, so it took immense concentration and time to truly comprehend what I was reading. I was more about learning from practical application, and there was no hands-on experience for macroeconomics. It was just dry, boring statistics that made my eyes glaze over.

I was down to my hardest college classes, and so close to obtaining my marketing degree so I could switch my internship at Dare PR for a full-time salaried position. As exhausting as it had been to juggle school, waitressing at The Back Door, and interning at Dare PR, there was definitely a light at the end of the tunnel and I couldn't wait to get there. But first, I had to get through my final exams coming up, which meant more studying. Ugh.

My shift at the bar tonight started at five, and after

texting Raven to see if I could talk to her beforehand, I wrapped up my studies and changed into my uniform—a pair of jeans and a T-shirt with The Back Door logo across the chest. I put my hair up into a ponytail, told Valerie I was heading out, and took the subway to the restaurant which was a much shorter ride from The Cortland than it took me from my old apartment.

I arrived with twenty minutes to spare before I had to clock in.

Admittedly, I was nervous about my upcoming conversation with Raven, for a few reasons. One, she was my best friend and I had to come clean about my night with her brother. Two, I had to explain how I'd become his fake girlfriend. And three, that I needed time off from work in order to fulfill that role.

My stomach twisted with anxiety as I walked into the bar from the back door—hence the name The Back Door—and headed toward where the office was located, which was where Raven usually was these days. She'd once worked the bar like me, but Remy preferred her doing the administrative part of the job now that they were married, and she seemed to enjoy it, as well.

Reaching the office, I knocked on the closed door, steeling myself for the discussion ahead.

"Go away," I heard Remy say, his voice gruff and annoyed.

"Come in," Raven said in a more breathless tone at the same time.

Since I'd asked for this meeting with Raven and figured she was expecting me, I followed her lead and opened the door. As I entered, I quickly realized why Remy hadn't wanted any interruptions. He was sitting behind the desk, with Raven on his lap, his hands just beneath the hem of her T-shirt and her face a little flushed. I was grateful that I hadn't walked in on something more risqué.

This wasn't the first time I'd caught them in a near-compromising position considering they couldn't keep their hands off each other, and since I had a great relationship with both of them, I didn't hesitate to lighten the moment.

"Oh, my God, you two. Get a room," I teased.

Remy grinned unrepentantly at me, still keeping Raven on his lap, who was biting her lower lip in embarrassment. "Last time I checked, this *was* a room," he retorted.

"Then next time, lock the damn door," I shot back cheekily.

He chuckled. "Noted." His gaze slid to the clock on the wall, then back to me. "Aren't you early for your shift?"

I nodded. "Yes, but I texted Raven and told her I needed to talk to her before my shift started."

"Uh, yes, she did," Raven clarified, still flustered. She slid off his thighs, and Remy reluctantly let her go. "Obviously, I got a little distracted."

"Doesn't take much, sweetheart," Remy said affectionately, and stood up.

I glanced away, not wanting to risk seeing just how much that *distraction* had affected him.

"We'll pick this up later," he said, and kissed Raven before heading out the door, closing it shut behind him.

"Good Lord, that man is so freaking full of himself," she said, laughing as she straightened her T-shirt and smoothed a hand over her slightly disheveled hair. "I'm so sorry about that."

I smiled. "The last thing you should apologize for is being married to a man who adores you."

"I know, I know. Have a seat," Raven said, indicating the chair in front of the desk as she settled into the one Remy had just vacated.

I did, and for the next few minutes we talked about Raven's birthday party that weekend. How genuinely surprised she'd been, and how much fun everyone seemed to have—all the while I kept thinking, how the hell was I going to tell Raven about the predicament I'd gotten myself into?

"So, what's up that you needed to come in early and talk to me?" she asked once that initial idle chit-chat was over.

I exhaled a deep breath, trying not to squirm in my chair from sheer awkwardness. "There's, umm, something important I need to tell you, and a request I need to make."

"You can relax, Stevie," she said, clearly seeing my discomfort. "I already know."

I stared at my friend, trying to read her expression,

trying to figure out what she was referring to. "You already know what?" I asked cautiously.

She leaned back in the leather chair and grimaced. "God, Caleb is going to kill me," she said beneath her breath.

"Or *I'm* going to kill *him*," I said through gritted teeth, suspecting that Caleb had already gotten to Raven before I had, which didn't make me happy. "What do you already know?"

"Please don't be mad at him," she said quickly, trying to ward off my displeasure. "I know Caleb only had good intentions—"

"What do you already know?" I asked for the third time, more sternly now so she'd quit beating around the bush.

She exhaled a deep breath. "He called me earlier and explained what happened with Alyssa yesterday morning, and how you're doing him a favor by being his pretend girlfriend for the next two months, until the custody case is over," she said in a rush to get it all out in the open. Then, a small smile curved her lips. "But let's be honest here...are things really fake between you two?"

"What do you mean?" I ask, not ready to admit to anything.

She arched a brow. "Clearly, you two hooked up Saturday night, in order for Alyssa to find you together the next morning. Which means you both finally gave in to the attraction you've been dancing around for the past year. There was nothing fake about that."

"It was only supposed to be one night," I said.

She laughed. "Caleb didn't sound all that upset that your *one night* was extended to two months."

"It's…a job," I argued, trying not to read too much into her comment. "He's *paying me* to be his girlfriend."

"As he should, since he roped you into it," she said, then grew serious. "He asked that tonight be your last shift until your arrangement ends, which isn't an issue if that's what *you* want since I have other waitresses wanting to pick up extra shifts. But I told him that was a presumptuous request to make on his part and also not his choice, since you might need the money and want to work the night shift longer."

"No," I said, and sighed, appreciating the fact that Raven hadn't automatically caved in to Caleb's demands. "Your brother is paying me very…generously. And also putting me up in one of his apartments at The Cortland."

Raven tapped her fingers on the desktop, her eyes gleaming with interest. "Well, that's convenient."

"Stop," I told her, not wanting her to get fanciful ideas in her head about Caleb and me. "It's not like that. He doesn't like where I live and feels it's safer for me, and Valerie, to be there for the time being."

"He's a really good guy, Stevie," Raven said softly. "He's also very…protective of those he cares about."

Now it was Raven who was making assumptions, because while I did think that Caleb worried about where I'd lived, *caring* for me was much too intimate of

CARLY PHILLIPS & ERIKA WILDE

a statement and not something I was willing to inter-
pret too deeply.

"I never said he wasn't a good guy," I said, focusing on that comment instead.

"I know...he just got screwed over by Alyssa, before the divorce, and now, again, with her using Owen
to fuck with his emotions," she said, upset on his
behalf. "Thank you for helping him out."

I tipped my head and gave her a half grin. "You do
realize that I wouldn't be in this predicament if he
hadn't volunteered me as his girlfriend, right?"

She gave me a saucy look. "And you do realize that
you wouldn't be in this predicament if the two of you
finally hadn't done the deed and gotten caught, right?"
she shot right back at me. "But you did, and I say
just...open yourself up to the possibilities."

That was easier said than done, because the last
thing I wanted to do was set myself up for potential
heartache. Raven got lucky with Remy, but rich,
successful men like Caleb didn't normally gravitate
toward women like me. When it came down to brass
tacks, Caleb and I were complete opposites, and I
didn't fit into his sophisticated, cultured world. Giving
in to our sexual attraction was one thing, but I wasn't
about to disillusion myself into believing that this
current situation of ours was anything more than a
business deal, as Caleb, himself, had stated.

I stood up, ready to change the topic. "I need to
get ready to start my shift. And thank you for being so
flexible about the next two months' leave. I appreciate

it."

Raven smiled. "Of course."

I left the office, clocked in, and headed to the bar area to start work. Customers were already streaming in, and while Mondays in general weren't as busy as the weekends, The Back Door always had a steady stream of customers every day of the week.

The next few hours passed quickly, and by nine I placed an order for a club sandwich then took my meal into the back room for my break. After eating a few bites, I pulled out my cellphone to make sure there weren't any messages from Valerie, and found one from Caleb instead, sent a few hours ago.

I'm picking you up after your shift tonight.

I pursed my lips, because his message was very matter-of-fact and direct, and he clearly expected me to agree because he'd said so. I wasn't a damsel, and I didn't need a white knight. I quickly replied with, *Thank you, but no, I'll take the subway. Just like I always have.*

I went back to eating my sandwich, expecting an argument from Caleb, but by the time my break was over and there was no reply from him, I assumed I'd made my point.

I acknowledged that I probably aggravated the hell out of Caleb with my independent streak, but growing up I'd learned that relying on anyone but myself outside of Valerie usually led to disappointment. I understood that Caleb was trying to make my life easier because he could, but I didn't want to get used to depending on him for anything more than what he'd already provided.

After living in New York City for three years, I knew how to watch out for myself. Was traveling on the subway at night unnerving at times? Absolutely. But I didn't expect Caleb to upend his life and his own routine for me.

The bar closed at eleven, and after those long hours on my feet I was exhausted. I spent another half an hour on cleanup and closing duties before I clocked out. I gathered my things from my locker and shrugged into my jacket as I walked back out into the dining area to find Caleb talking to Remy.

Of course he was here.

Remy saw me first. "Hey, looks like your ride is here," he said jovially.

Caleb had the nerve to grin at me, and it so wasn't fair that he looked so sexy in a pair of dark wash jeans and a lightweight sweater that showcased his wide shoulders and chest. While I knew I looked like a hot mess with strands of hair falling out of my ponytail and splotches on my T-shirt from spilled drinks, and I probably smelled like greasy burgers and French fries.

"I didn't order a rideshare," I said, squaring my shoulders and looking Caleb in the eye.

He shrugged. "I was in the neighborhood and figured I might as well offer you a ride back to the apartment since I was heading in that direction anyway."

A blatant lie at this hour, clearly, and I almost laughed at how believable he made it sound. "Oh, now you're *offering*?" I asked, arching a brow. "Not demanding?"

His expression turned serious, when I'd expected him to make light of the situation. "The tone of your last text came through loud and clear, so yes, this is me offering, and not demanding."

"Remy! Can you help me with this keg of beer?" Raven called out from the liquor room in the back.

"Coming," he said, heading in that direction and leaving me alone with Caleb.

Once Remy was gone, Caleb strolled toward me. "There is something I do want to say, so listen up, sweetheart," he said, coming to a stop in front of me. Touching his warm fingers beneath my chin, he tipped my head back so I was looking into his gorgeous blue eyes. "Two months is going to be a long time if we keep butting heads, which is the last thing I want to do. But if something happened to you on my watch, I'd never forgive myself. So, as stubborn and self-reliant as you are, which I definitely admire, try and cut me a little slack for wanting to make sure you get home safely, okay?"

The last of my annoyance deflated out of me. For one thing, I was too tired to be upset. And another, I couldn't deny that there was something sweet about Caleb's insistence when I'd never had anyone so concerned about my welfare. But I also hated disrupting his evening, especially when I knew it was his week with Owen...which made me wonder where his son was.

"Where is Owen?" I asked curiously.

"At home. In bed," Caleb said, gently brushing back a stray strand of my hair from my face. "Cara is there right now. She's mostly a night owl and I told her I wouldn't be long."

I offered him a smile as a truce. "Well, then let's get going."

I followed him out back to where his car was parked. Once we were buckled inside, he navigated his way through the city while I let my weary body sink into the plush leather seat. Begrudgingly, I had to admit that his car was much more comfortable, and safer, than the subway, and I relaxed and let myself enjoy the ride.

After a short while, I turned my head to look at Caleb, his handsome profile illuminated by the city lights outside his window. "You'll be happy to know that tonight is my last night at The Back Door until our arrangement is over, but I would appreciate you not making any assumptions on my behalf going forward."

He was quiet for a moment, then gave a nod and glanced my way. "You're right. And I'm sorry."

Well...that was easy. No excuses, but an apology. Which went a long way in soothing my pride. Caleb might have overprotective, caveman tendencies, but as Raven had stated earlier, he was a man with good intentions.

He parked his car in his designated spot in the underground garage, then walked with me to the elevators. I swiped my key card and pressed the number for my floor. As we headed upward, I realized that this particular elevator didn't have access to the penthouse level, so I was surprised when we arrived on my floor and Caleb didn't step out of the lift with me.

I stopped and glanced back at him, and he merely smiled at me.

"Have a good day at work tomorrow," he said.

I nodded. "You, too."

And that was it. The doors closed and I walked toward my apartment, realizing that he'd taken the time to really make sure I'd gotten home safely, out of respect and kindness. There were no expectations other than that, despite the money he was paying me, and the luxurious apartment he'd set me and Valerie up in for the next two months.

I couldn't deny the light fluttering sensation in my chest, or the realization that *not* falling for Caleb Kane was going to be more difficult than I'd imagined.

CHAPTER TEN

Caleb

I GLANCED AT my watch as my good friend and business partner, Beck Daniels, talked about the commercial property in Hudson Yards he'd sold to a developer that was now being turned into a retail space with high-end shops, flagship stores, and at least two new fine dining establishments. I was listening and even interjecting comments and questions where appropriate, but clearly I was distracted by tonight's plans with Stevie.

It wasn't anything elaborate or fancy, but the thought of spending time with her, in any capacity, had me anticipating the night ahead.

"Why do you keep checking your watch?" Beck asked, sounding more amused than annoyed as he sat across his desk from where I was seated. "Am I boring you, or do you have a hot date with your new girl-friend?"

Other than Raven, Beck was the only person I'd told about what had happened with Alyssa and my arrangement with Stevie, only because he was well aware that I'd had no love life to speak of for the past two years, and to go from zero to sixty in the span of a weekend with any woman was suspect, and unrealistic.

"I invited her to my place to have dinner with Owen and me," I said, shifting in my seat. "I told her seven, so I need to head out soon."

"Sounds very domestic," Beck said humorously. "Kind of like my life."

"You have a great life," I replied, which was true.

"I do," he agreed, and grinned. "A gorgeous wife to go home to. A daughter who has me wrapped around her finger. I know that I usually try to get out of the office at a reasonable time, but I don't think I've ever seen you so anxious to leave work."

I shrugged, because the feeling was definitely new for me. "Other than my time with Owen, I've never had a reason to want to leave early."

Beck sat up in his chair. "Okay, then let's wrap things up and get out of here."

As Beck cleared his desk, I stood up. "As you know, Gerard Laurent is flying in from the UK next week to discuss purchasing that triplex penthouse at Central Park Tower. We have dinner on the books with him and his wife, and you mentioned Chloe will be there, so I'll invite Stevie since I'm usually the odd man out at these things with no date."

Beck grinned. "I'm sure Chloe will enjoy having her there."

We headed down to the parking garage together and parted ways. I drove home, definitely anxious to see Stevie. I'd seen her briefly Monday night after picking her up from The Back Door, but yesterday she'd worked at Dare PR and as much as I wanted to spend time with her, or invite her over in the evening, I'd given her space since I knew I'd be seeing her tonight.

I'd known her for a year, but now that we'd crossed that line and slept together, something had changed for me. There was no more resisting temptation, and now I found myself thinking about her all the time, and crazily enough, missing her smiles. Her easy humor. And yes, even that feisty side to her personality.

One of the things I liked and appreciated about Stevie was that I always knew where I stood with her. She didn't let things that were bothering her fester to the point that they built resentment, which had been Alyssa's style of resolving conflict, along with giving me the cold shoulder. With Stevie, I was quickly learning that if she had an issue with something, she spoke her mind.

Her dynamic personality was stimulating and arousing…though the latter I'd had to keep in check. As much as I would have loved fixing a few of our differences of opinion with hot, hard makeup sex, that hadn't been an option. I had Owen to think of, at least until Sunday when he'd be off to Alyssa's for a week and I'd be alone again.

I arrived home at ten after six, which gave me time to relieve Tillie, the elderly widowed woman in the building who I'd hired to pick up Owen after school and watch him until I made it home from work.

I changed into jeans and a casual long-sleeved Henley, and while Owen sat at the kitchen counter and finished the last of his homework on his laptop, I started prepping dinner. Or rather, warming up what Marcel had made for tonight's meal.

Even though I'd given Stevie a key card to my penthouse the day she'd moved in so she'd have access and could have arrived unannounced, she texted me that she was on her way up. A few minutes later I heard the soft ping of the elevator.

Owen glanced in that direction, his eyes lighting up when he saw Stevie since we didn't get many guests other than Cara. He jumped off his stool and ran toward her, his excitement making me grin because I felt the same damn way.

"Stevie! Guess what?" Owen said enthusiastically. "We're having spaghetti and garlic bread for dinner!"

"Really? That's my favorite," she replied, her voice animated for his benefit as they headed toward the kitchen. "It smells amazing and I'm starved. Oh, and I brought dessert. I made some brownies."

She met my gaze and I smirked, unable to resist teasing her. "What? No chocolate mousse?"

Her face flushed adorably. I walked around the counter to greet her and placed a soft kiss on her cheek. I told myself it was because I wanted Owen to get used to seeing a little PDA between the two of us, but the truth of the matter was, I just liked touching

Stevie and being close to her. It was all I could do not to pull her into my arms and kiss her like I *really* wanted to.

She gave me a wide-eyed, startled look. "You're just full of surprises, aren't you?" she murmured.

"You have no idea," I replied, and chuckled.

She set the plate of brownies on the counter and regained her composure. "What can I do to help?"

"Everything is ready and just needs to be put on the table. While Owen and I do that, you can pour us a glass of wine," I said, indicating the bottle of Chianti I'd set out.

She picked up the bottle and looked at the private label, then arched a brow my way at the obviously expensive wine. "This is very fancy for Chianti," she murmured.

"Yes, so enjoy it."

We all worked together, Owen and I taking the salad, garlic bread, and Marcel's spaghetti bolognese to the table, and Stevie following with our wine, as well as a glass of milk for Owen.

We sat down at the dining table, plated our dishes, and after a few bites I glanced at Stevie.

"Since you had today off from the PR firm, did you do anything fun?" I asked.

She grimaced. "I wish. More studying and home-work. With finals coming up next month, it's getting intense."

"You have homework, too?" Owen asked, his eyes wide with surprise.

"I do," she said after taking a sip of her wine, then grinned at Owen. "Macroeconomics is the worst."

Owen scrunched up his face. "What is macro…" The rest of the word was a garbled, indecipherable attempt at repeating the term.

Stevie laughed, the sound light and amused. "It's sort of like math, but super boring and makes me want to take a nap."

I chuckled. "So, what degree are you pursuing?" I asked, curious to know, well, everything I could about her.

"One in marketing," she said, twirling her spaghetti noodles around the tines of her fork. "I've been interning at Dare PR for a little over a year now, and my boss has already promised me that they'll hire me full-time once I finish school, which will enable me to quit waitressing and have one job that pays me well."

I couldn't help but admire how hard she was working to build a secure future for herself. "And what, exactly, do you do at Dare PR?"

"Anything and everything PR related," she said with a light laugh. "Advertising and promotions for clients, of course, but right now I'm working on a social media campaign for a specific client, focusing mainly on branding and content creation."

The unfettered enthusiasm in her voice and sparkle in her eye as she talked about Dare PR told me that she loved what she did.

"And what about you?" she asked, turning the subject to me. "Any big real estate sales lately?"

"There's always something in the works," I said, and realized this was a perfect opening for next week's dinner with Gerard Laurent. "Next Wednesday, I'd like to bring you with me to a business dinner with one of our biggest clients. If all goes well, he'll be purchasing a triplex penthouse at Central Park Tower, so a little schmoozing is in order."

"Are you sure?" She fiddled nervously with the stem of her wineglass, looking uneasy. "I mean, I'm not sure why you'd need me there."

Need? No. "How about it's as simple as I want you there."

"I think that's a little outside of my comfort zone."

"You're my girlfriend, so consider it part of the job," I said, then gentled my tone when I saw the genuine insecurities in her gaze. "All you need to do is be yourself, Stevie. And Beck's wife, Chloe, will be there, too. I know she'll enjoy your company. There're a few other events I'll be taking you to, as well, so we'll discuss those later. I'm just glad not to have to attend them solo anymore."

She exhaled a deep breath. "Sounds like I'm going to need a social calendar to keep track of everything."

"And don't forget my birthday!" Owen chimed in. "I'm going to be seven!"

"When is your birthday?" Stevie asked, smiling at him. "Because that is something I definitely don't want to miss."

"It's…It's…" A frown furrowed between Owen's brows as he glanced at me. "When is it again, Dad?"

"In a few weeks," I told him.

Owen huffed. "You said that *last* time."

"That's because it's still in a few weeks," I tried to explain, knowing that probably seemed like a lifetime to a child.

"Oh." He thought about that for a moment, then his eyes lit up again as he looked at Stevie. "We're going to the beach for my birthday!"

"That sounds like fun," she said, then finished off the last of her Chianti.

"It's a small family weekend planned at the Hamptons," I explained. "I have a membership at the Dune Deck Beach Club and it'll be Remy and Raven and Cara, and us."

"Oh." Her eyes widened, and she gave her head a slight shake. "Then you should all go and have a nice getaway. I don't need to be there."

Owen pouted. "But I want you there."

"And so do I," I said, for more reasons than just the pretense of being my girlfriend at a resort where Alyssa was also still a member, which she'd insisted on as part of the divorce settlement.

I recognized the uncertainty in her eyes. "Where would I stay?"

I knew she was asking because of the morality clause, and it still being an issue of her staying overnight with me when I was with Owen, even if she was my girlfriend. "You can room with Cara. I'll book a two-bedroom suite for you and her to stay in." She opened her mouth, and I cut off whatever she intended to say. "No arguments, and who wants a brownie with ice cream?" I asked, knowing that would put an end to the subject.

"I do, I do!" Owen shouted, right on cue.

"Then help me clear the table and we'll have dessert," I promised him.

We all worked together in the kitchen, with Owen clearing the dishes while Stevie rinsed them and stacked them in the dishwasher, and I put away the leftovers. Brownies came next, with scoops of vanilla ice cream while Owen regaled Stevie about his day at school.

Our nightly routine continued, followed by a quick game of Owen's choice, and tonight he picked Trash Pandas, a fun racoon card game that had us all laughing because it was absolutely ridiculous, but right on par for a six-year-old.

"It's almost eight o'clock," I told Owen once we'd finished the game. "You need a bath and then it's time for bed."

"Do I have to? I like having Stevie here. She's fun."

"I agree, but yes, you have to," I said, ruffling his hair. "You have school tomorrow."

"Okay." He slid off his chair, then looked hopefully at Stevie. "Will you read one of my books to me tonight, instead of Dad?"

She smiled. "Sure."

I ushered Owen off for a bath while Stevie waited in the living room and scrolled through her phone to pass time. Once Owen was in his pajamas and settled in bed, I called Stevie back to his bedroom. She came in and sat down next to him.

"I made sure he picked a short story," I told her, leaning against Owen's dresser. "Because if not, you'd be reading to him for an hour."

"I want you to read this one," Owen said, handing her a book.

Stevie glanced at the cover and grinned. "Okay, *Grumpy Monkey* it is."

She started to read, and I wasn't sure who enjoyed Stevie's narration more, my son or myself. The inflections in her voice to emulate the grumpy monkey, along with her humorous expressions, had Owen laughing and me chuckling.

When she was done, I tucked the covers around Owen, left his night-light on, and closed his bedroom door on our way out.

We walked back out to the living area. "So, you've just experienced a very ordinary evening in the life of me with my son."

"It was fun," she said, picking up her purse from the counter. "But I should go. I've got work in the morning."

I nodded. I didn't want her to leave, but I understood. Everything about the past few hours had been casual, easy, and enjoyable. It also made me realize how much I missed having the companionship of a woman in our lives on a daily basis. One who melded into our routine, instead of disrupting it as Alyssa always had.

I walked with her to the elevator, but before she could press the button I gently grabbed her wrist. She glanced at me, blinking in surprise, but I also saw the shimmer of awareness in her eyes, as if she knew why I'd stopped her.

"Hang on," I murmured and lifted my hand, cradling the side of her face and wrapping my other arm around her waist, bringing her body flush to mine. "There's something I've been dying to do since you walked in earlier."

Placing her hands on my chest, she licked her bottom lip, anticipation flickering in her gaze. "Whatever it is, you need to keep it PG."

"I'll try," I said, my voice low and husky as I dipped my head down to hers.

Seconds later, my mouth touched hers, and her lips automatically parted on a soft sigh of invitation that I took full advantage of, seeking her tongue with my own. Now that I knew what it was like to kiss her, what she tasted like, I craved this connection with her constantly and took full advantage of the fact that I had her in my arms, if only for a short amount of time.

I kept the kiss slow and hot and deep, the kind that was seductive as hell and made my dick stiffen and ache to be inside of her. Her fingers curled into my Henley, enticing sounds escaping her as she shifted her hips against mine, rubbing against my rigid cock.

Knowing I was on the verge of hoisting her over my shoulder, like the caveman she claimed me to be, and hauling her off to my bedroom where I could fuck her over the next few hours—which wasn't a possibility with Owen in the house—I lifted my mouth from hers and reluctantly ended the kiss.

She whimpered softly, feeling the loss as profoundly as I did, and pressed her forehead to mine. "I need to go because you are much too tempting, as is *this*." Her hand slid over my erection and gave it a firm squeeze.

I groaned and instinctively pushed my dick against her palm, tormenting myself with what I couldn't have and disappointed that it would likely be *my* hand stroking my dick tonight, and not hers.

"You're going to pay for that the next time we're completely alone."

A sinful smile tipped up the corners of her lips. "I hope so."

I gave her a soft, chaste kiss this time, and stepped back while I still could, pressing the button to the elevator. "Good night, sweetheart."

The doors opened, and she stepped inside, then turned around to face me, her face beautifully flushed and her lips pink and slightly swollen from our kiss. "Good night, Caleb."

CHAPTER ELEVEN

Stevie

"ALL RIGHT, TEAM," Jack, one of the senior PR managers at Dare PR, said, addressing the small group sitting in the conference room, including myself. "Our main goal with PureGlow Cosmetics is to boost their brand awareness and drive engagement on social media. Their core message is all about inclusivity and natural beauty. Stevie, as content creator, what ideas have you come up with to support that?"

All eyes turned to me. This team was a small one with four of us in total, but I could still remember the first time that had happened, how intimidated and full of nerves I'd been to have more experienced strategists staring expectantly at me. But after a year at this firm and working with these people who I highly respected, and vice versa, I was much more confident in my abilities and sharing my ideas.

I had my detailed notes in front of me on the table, but I'd immersed myself in this campaign and knew my selling points by heart and didn't need them.

"We've discussed reaching a diverse demographic for PureGlow and I believe video content on social media is going to be huge in reaching those target groups," I said, clasping my hands on the table and glancing at each person in turn. "TikTok, Instagram Reels, and even YouTube Shorts would be perfect for showcasing how their products work, especially in real life scenarios. People love seeing transformations or before-and-after shots. But I also think incorporating a good, emotional story will draw in potential buyers. It will also help foster relationships for PureGlow and build trust."

"Agreed," Kyle, one of the brand managers, chimed in. "It's all about creating a community for PureGlow and that's a great start."

I nodded, getting more excited about these concepts I'd come up with. "In terms of community, how about starting a hashtag campaign? Something like '#NaturalAndInclusive' or '#BeautyForAll'? We could encourage followers to share their own stories and experiences with the products using the hashtags. We could even share some of the best user stories and offer giveaways to build buzz."

"I love that idea," Sarah said, her tone full of enthusiasm as she stood up and walked to the whiteboard in the room, prepared to jot down notes. "That would create a lot of user-generated content, which is a great way to get more reach and build organic awareness for the client. What else have we got?"

From there, the four of us spent the rest of the morning brainstorming all the unique and different ways we could engage viewers. By the time we were done, we had a whiteboard filled with strategies, over half of which were mine.

"Great job today," Jack said, once Sarah and Kyle were out of the conference room and I was still gathering my written notes. "Your ideas were solid. I especially like the one about integrating regular challenges, like that thirty-day skin care challenge using the product line that you suggested. Daily prompts on various social media channels and having users tag the brand and other friends to join in on the challenge was a brilliant idea."

Jack and I had a great working relationship, and his praise always boosted my confidence. "Thank you. I spent a lot of time working on developing those ideas."

"And it shows." He grinned, tossing his empty paper coffee cup into the trash. "You're going to be a great asset to Dare PR once Samantha puts you in a full-time position."

Jack turned his head as someone walked by the conference room, the walls of which were built with floor-to-ceiling glass partitions. I followed his gaze, seeing Brandy chatting easily with my sister as Brandy led her to her corner office for the interview Valerie had today at eleven.

Jack blatantly stared at Valerie, interest flickering in his eyes as he craned his neck to keep watching them as they continued down the hallway.

Amusement trickled through me. "Would you mind taking your eyes off my sister's ass?"

Startled, Jack immediately straightened and glanced at me, his face flushing red. "Your sister?"

"Yes." I opened my phone and used my camera to take a picture of the notes on the whiteboard to use later when I put together the final presentation for the client. "She's here today to interview as Brandy's new assistant."

He grinned, smoothing a hand down his silk tie. "Is she single?"

I looked at Jack, who was one of those classically handsome kind of guys. A little nerdy, but intelligent, and most importantly, a genuinely nice and kind person. That's all I'd ever seen in the year of working with him. However, after what Valerie had gone through with Mark, I couldn't deny feeling a little protective of her, which ironically reminded me of Caleb's behavior with me, not that I was going to analyze that too closely.

"You don't even know her," I said to Jack, though I was smiling.

He shrugged. "Hey, a strong initial attraction is the most important part of getting to know someone."

When I thought about the crazy chemistry between myself and Caleb that had been there from day one, I conceded his point. "Yes, she's single, but she just went through a bad breakup and she's a little…guarded."

"Got it," Jack said, his expression surprisingly serious. "So, don't move too fast and overwhelm her. But asking her out for a coffee or lunch is pretty harmless, right?"

"Sure." If Valerie was going to dip her toe back into the dating pool, someone easygoing and trustworthy like Jack was a good place to start.

I gathered up the rest of my things, as did Jack, and we left the conference room together, heading down the hallway in the opposite direction of Brandy's office.

"Maybe you could introduce us sometime," Jack said, his mind still on Valerie. "If she doesn't get hired on as Brandy's assistant."

And if she did get hired …well, luckily there wasn't any policy against interoffice romances. "We'll see," I replied, giving him a cheeky grin as we parted ways when we reached his office, one that came with a view of Manhattan as senior PR manager.

I returned to my small cubicle, which was also separated by glass partitions, so I was able to see when Brandy walked with Valerie back out to the reception area a while later. They were both smiling as they talked, but I couldn't get a read on how well the interview might have gone.

Luckily, I was meeting Valerie for lunch in fifteen minutes at the deli right next to the office building. At noon, I let Jack know I was heading out for a bite to eat, anxious to hear all the details. I walked into the deli, grateful that my sister had already secured us a table since it was lunch hour, and slid into the chair across from her. Two iced teas had already been delivered, along with two settings, so I knew Valerie had already ordered for the both of us.

I looked at her, but she wore an annoyingly good poker face. "Well?" I asked, exasperated that she was giving me nothing to go on.

Her face broke into a grin and she nearly shrieked, "I got the job!"

I laughed, loving her excitement and beyond ecstatic for her. "Oh my God, that's fantastic!"

Valerie beamed. "I know, right? I didn't think I'd walk out of there with a job, but Brandy said she'd interviewed a few people already, and she really liked what was on my résumé in terms of my previous duties as an assistant…even after I told her what had happened with Mark. She was actually very sympathetic about the situation, like you said she'd probably be. At the end of the interview, she made me an offer that was more than my last job and I start on Monday!"

I grinned, her elation infectious. "I'm so happy for you." I picked up my iced tea and raised it toward her. "Cheers to you."

She clinked her glass to mine, just as our lunch order arrived. Salads for both of us and I ate a few bites before speaking again.

"So, I'm giving you a heads-up that you already have an admirer at the office," I told my sister.

Intrigue touched her expression. "Oh?"

I nodded. "Yep. His name is Jack. He's the senior

PR manager. He's a solid guy. And a gentleman, other than the fact that he was staring at your ass when you walked by the conference room."

Valerie giggled, her eyes sparkling happily. "A nice, unspoken compliment. I'll take it."

"Don't be surprised if he asks you out for coffee or lunch once you start at the office." I stabbed a piece of chicken with my fork. "And I can vouch for him. He's a very easygoing and an all-around nice guy. He's successful, without an overinflated ego. In other words, no drama."

She arched a brow at me. "Then why aren't *you* dating him?"

I shrugged. "Because he's not my type." Which was true.

"Oh, right," Valerie said, her tone filled with humor. "Hot billionaires with big dick energy are."

I rolled my eyes at her. "Jack and I have a great working relationship, but that's it. He's clearly interested in you, so if you're anywhere near ready to try dating again, he's someone I'd trust."

She bit her bottom lip, seemingly considering that. "I can do a lunch, or coffee, and see how it goes."

I was glad to see my sister opening up again, relieved that Mark hadn't completely crushed her self-esteem.

We continued eating lunch while I gave her a rundown of my meeting today and how well it had gone. When we were finished, we headed out of the deli and I waited at the curb with her, chitchatting until her rideshare arrived to take her back to the apartment.

Her cellphone rang and she dug it out of her purse. An unfamiliar number was on the display, which usually indicated a spam call.

She looked hesitant, because nobody enjoyed dealing with telemarketers. "I should answer this just in case it's Brandy or someone at Dare PR about my employment starting on Monday."

I agreed. I knew that calls from the office always showed up with the firm's name for me, but considering Valerie had just been offered the job, I understood why she didn't want to ignore the incoming call.

She connected the line and put the phone to her ear. "Hello?"

"Where the fuck are you?" Mark yelled so loud, even I could hear him.

Valerie froze, and I saw the immediate panic and fear transform her expression.

"You haven't been at the apartment for days," he went on, screaming like a lunatic and giving away the fact that he'd been stalking her again. "And don't think that I can't find you, wherever you are!"

My sister seemed paralyzed, in shock and unable to respond or move so I grabbed the phone from her. "Leave her the fuck alone," I said, furious that he'd dare to break the restraining order and find a way to call her anonymously. Not to mention his threats. "She's done with you, asshole!"

"Yeah, well, maybe I'm not done with her." Suddenly, he huffed out a breath, as if realizing how unhinged he sounded, and tried a more reasonable tactic. "Look, all I want is to talk to her. And apologize."

My stomach churned at those words, familiar ones that reminded me of the way our father had always groveled his way back into our mother's good graces. How he'd given her false hopes and promises that things would be better this time around. Except they never were, and the abuse only escalated until…well, I refused to think of that outcome for Valerie.

Valerie seemed to regain her composure enough to take the phone back. "I don't want your apology, Mark," she said, her voice stronger than I'd anticipated, making me proud of her resolve in the moment. "I want you to just stay out of my life. Stop calling me. It's against the restraining order and I'm going to report you to the police."

"Wherever you are, I'm going to find you," he said, his tone intimidating.

Refusing to allow the prick any more airtime to terrorize my sister, I grabbed Valerie's phone and disconnected the call and quickly restricted the new number.

Despite Valerie's bit of bravado, I could see that she was shaking, her eyes filled with shock as we stood there on the sidewalk and pedestrians walked around us.

"How?" she whispered, shaking her head in confusion. "I blocked his number."

"He clearly used a burner phone to try and trick

you." I tamped down my anger and forced a calm I didn't feel. "You're fine, Valerie," I reassured her. "No one at our old apartment knows where we are, and we're safe in the new one."

She swallowed hard and wrapped her arms around her midsection. "I just want him to leave me alone."

My heart ached for her. "Don't respond. Don't answer any more calls from a number you don't recognize. He'll get bored and move on." I knew it wasn't a promise I could stand by, but it was all I had right now to try and keep her from completely freaking out.

"I know," she said, though she didn't look completely convinced. "I just want it to be sooner, rather than later, so I can move on with my life."

"You already are." I smiled at her. "You've already got a new job, and we are not moving back to the old apartment when I'm done with Caleb. We clearly can't afford a place at The Cortland, but I can now afford a building with security and a doorman in a safer area."

She nodded, finally looking more reassured and mollified. "And I can help pay the rent, too, now that I have a new job with a better salary than the one I had before."

I forced a smile for her benefit. "We'll figure everything out. I promise."

Her phone pinged, and Valerie visibly startled, until I checked her messages to see that her rideshare had arrived and was waiting at the curb a few car lengths up. I walked with her to the vehicle and she slid inside.

"Text me when you get home," I told her.

"I will," she promised.

I watched her car drive away, then obsessively checked my messages, waiting to hear from her. I didn't relax until she finally assured me she was safe in our apartment.

CHAPTER TWELVE

Caleb

O N SATURDAY, A week after Alyssa had caught Stevie and I together in the kitchen, I took Owen to visit my mother. These visits were never pleasant for me but I tried not to let my strained relationship with her affect her spending time with her only grandchild. As I sat across from Cassandra, she grilled me about Alyssa, as my ex had already told her everything that had happened with Stevie, embellishing the situation and turning it into something sordid.

She didn't bother disguising her disapproval of my life, not that I gave a shit what she thought of anyone I dated. Luckily, Owen was playing ball in the nearby backyard with my mother's corgi, oblivious to the grown-up tension.

"I just don't understand why you won't at least try and reconcile with Alyssa," my mother said from her seat on the patio. "She's trying so hard. She's completely clean now and Owen should have both of his parents under one roof."

I slanted her an incredulous look. "First of all,

there will be no reconciling with Alyssa, ever. There's too much that happened between us that I will never be okay with. And she *should* be drug-free, for Owen's sake if not for her own."

My mother's lips pursed. "She made a few mistakes. Everyone does. That doesn't mean they can't be forgiven." Her pointed look let me know she wasn't just talking about Alyssa.

A muscle in my jaw clenched. "Like Lance?" I asked, since I refused to have any type of relationship with my sociopathic twin. "You're making excuses for Alyssa the same way you do for him. Lance is in prison for a reason."

She huffed indelicately. "One simple mistake shouldn't ruin his whole life."

One simple mistake? More like half a dozen violent crimes, but I didn't bother correcting her. "So, it doesn't matter how many lives he's destroyed?"

My mother opened her mouth to speak, and I immediately cut her off. "Never mind. We're never going to agree on this issue. Not on Lance, and not on Alyssa."

I abruptly stood up, having reached my limit of patience. "Owen and I need to go. I promised him I'd take him to his favorite pizza place for lunch." I glanced out to the backyard, where Owen was still tossing the ball for the dog. "Hey, buddy! Time to go."

He came running over, and I honestly hated that there was nothing about these visits that Owen enjoyed. Cassandra wasn't the warm, loving grandmother he deserved and even the hug that she gave him now was stiff and more obligatory than a true affectionate embrace. It was times like this that I missed my father, who was dead and gone. Growing up, he'd been so much warmer and more affectionate than my mother, and he would have adored Owen.

"Will I get to see him for his birthday?" my mother asked as she followed us through her house to the front door. "It's just not the same now that you and Alyssa don't throw him a big party with all our friends there."

Those spectacles had been Alyssa's doing, putting together a ridiculously huge and expensive bash for a kid that was all for show and appearances, thrown only to impress her friends and make sure everyone knew that money was no object. I'd hated those parties, which was why I'd changed things up with Owen's birthdays once Alyssa and I divorced.

"I'm taking him to the beach club for his birthday weekend, just like I have the past few years. I'll make sure you get to see him sometime that week before we go."

"Will your…girlfriend be there?" she asked, her tone already dripping with criticism at the word *girlfriend*.

"Yes, Stevie is going," I said, but made sure my mother knew what the arrangements would be because she'd no doubt report back to Alyssa. "She'll be staying with Cara in her suite."

By the time I left, I was mentally fried and worked

up at the same time, and when we returned home after stopping for lunch, I wasn't in the best mood and needed to decompress. I called to see if Cara was around and asked her to watch Owen while I spent the next two hours in the downstairs gym, working off my aggression.

On Sunday, I handed off Owen to Alyssa.

The next three days until I had plans to see Stevie for my business dinner passed at a snail's pace. The time since I'd seen her last had most definitely *not* flown by. I couldn't get Stevie out of my mind. Not when I was at home, not when I was at work, and most certainly not when I was in my bed alone at night and wished she were there with me.

Every night one or the other of us had been busy, which didn't stop us from texting each other about our days—and flirting—because if I couldn't be with her in person, I found myself wanting to connect with her in other ways until I was able to see her for tonight's dinner with Beck and Chloe, and Gerard Laurent and his wife, Hazel.

After a too long day at the office—though an incredibly productive one since Gerard and his wife had submitted an offer on the triplex penthouse at Central Park Tower, which made tonight's dinner more of a celebratory event—I arrived home and took a shower and changed into a fresh suit.

Finally, Stevie was all mine. I wasn't thrilled that we had a long, drawn-out meal and pleasantries to sit through, but once that was over I had every intention of making up for lost time. As in, bringing her back to my apartment afterward, stripping her naked, and keeping her *very* busy in my bed for the rest of the night.

At six-thirty, I knocked on Stevie's door to pick her up.

She answered, her eyes bright with excitement and a wide smile on her lips. She called out to Valerie that she was leaving, and I walked with her to the elevator. Once we were inside and heading down, she smoothed a hand along the front of her silky black dress that was subtly sexy, skimming her body just enough for me to appreciate her sensual curves.

"I hope I dressed appropriately for the restaurant we're going to?"

The question was tinged with a hint of self-conscious uncertainty that she had no reason to feel. I took in the complete package…the way she'd worn her hair up in a more elegant style, her smoky eye makeup and daring choice of lip color, then continued down to the classic, sophisticated black dress and tasteful heels that completed the ensemble.

"You look gorgeous," I said, meaning it, and followed that up with a sinful smile. "The only thing that would make you look even more beautiful is if you weren't wearing anything at all."

A pink blush suffused her cheeks, but her eyes shone with awareness. "So, that's how it's going to go tonight, huh?"

"Me imagining you naked?" I asked, turning toward her and closing the very short distance between us, until her back was pressed against the cool chrome interior wall. "Absolutely," I murmured.

I lifted my hand and stroked the backs of my fingers along the side of her bare neck, watching with satisfaction as she shivered from my touch. "In fact, all throughout dinner, I'm going to be thinking about pulling those pins from this fancy updo so I can wrap your hair around my fist while I fuck you."

Her eyes darkened with desire as they looked up into mine, and her lips parted on a soft exhale of breath.

I smiled, skimming my thumb along her chin, not done seducing her imagination that would hopefully keep her on edge until we were alone later. "But first, before I do that, I'm going to put you on your knees because that red lipstick you're wearing? It's a goddamn tease and I want to see it smeared all over my cock while you suck my dick."

A small groan escaped her throat, even while she tried to maintain her composure by raising a brow at me. "You've *very* presumptuous, Mr. Kane."

"No, not presumptuous at all," I said, lifting my gaze from those tempting lips. "Just very confident, and now, for the rest of the night, you're going to think of all those things, too."

"You're not playing fair at all," she whispered, but it wasn't a complaint.

"It's been a long, excruciating week and a half since I had the pleasure of fucking you. A week and a half of fantasizing all the dirty, filthy things I want to do to you, and tonight, I plan to indulge. Unless…you'd rather not?"

She gave her head a quick shake, as if she didn't want to give me the chance to change my mind. "I didn't say that."

I chuckled, the sound a little devious. "Didn't think so."

The elevator dinged its arrival, and as the doors slid open I placed a soft, chaste kiss on her cheek so I didn't mess up that sexy-as-sin lipstick. I took her hand in mine and walked with her through the lobby, not missing the glances a few men cast her way that made me feel territorial as hell.

Stevie seemed oblivious to those stares. She honestly had no idea how appealing she was. How sexy but also unassuming and sweet, with a just enough tenacity to keep things interesting. It was a combination I found irresistible.

My driver, Dylan, was already parked and waiting in the valet area for us, and since we weren't alone I behaved and kept our conversation casual on the way to the restaurant. I caught up on how her campaign was going at Dare PR that she seemed so excited about, we discussed her latest macroeconomics test which she'd passed, and Stevie filled me in on Valerie's first few days at the firm and how much her sister was enjoying her new job.

We arrived at Mastro's Steakhouse the same time that Beck and his wife, Chloe, did, and a few minutes later Gerard and Hazel joined us. Introductions were made for the women, then the hostess led us through an upscale dining area to a private room I'd had my assistant reserve for the six of us so we'd have a much quieter and more intimate experience.

Wine was ordered and poured while we perused the menu, and once everyone's orders were taken, general conversation ensued. Since most of the day had been spent focused on business with Gerard, the men gravitated toward discussing more personal interests, like sports and current events.

Chloe and Stevie hit it off immediately, which didn't surprise me at all. As soon as Chloe learned that Stevie worked at The Back Door, they realized they had acquaintances in common since Chloe was a Kingston, and her sister, Aurora, was married to a Dare...which connected them to Zach Dare, who was half owner of The Back Door.

"Wait a second," Stevie said, her eyes lighting up as realization struck. "You're a Kingston, as in related to Dash Kingston, the rock star?"

Chloe nodded, smiling as she took a sip of her wine. "Yes, that's my brother."

"I have to confess, I might have had a slight fangirl moment when I first heard his music," Stevie said, then laughed. "Okay, who am I kidding? I still do."

As the two continued to chat, drawing Hazel into their conversation, I listened in on Gerard and Beck's debate about golf, which was my least favorite sport, so I didn't have much to contribute.

Our meals arrived, and surprisingly, the next few hours passed quickly. After dessert we all parted ways, and when Stevie and I were seated in the back of my SUV and heading home while Dylan drove, I glanced over at her, seeing how quiet and thoughtful she looked.

"Did you have a nice evening?" I asked, placing my hand on her knee.

She turned her head and smiled at me. "I did. It was quite different than I thought it would be."

I raised a brow, curious to know what she meant. "How so?"

She bit her bottom lip for a few seconds, then her eyes met mine, clear and direct, but I didn't miss the touch of hesitation there. "You want honesty?"

I nodded. "Always. Good or bad, I appreciate the truth, and there's nothing you could ever say that would offend me."

There was a slight pause before she exhaled, almost like she was deciding how much to reveal. "I was nervous going into this dinner, and self-conscious," she admitted, which I'd already suspected. "I mean, being in that kind of upscale restaurant was intimidating enough, let alone meeting women I didn't know and having no idea if we'd connect, especially with Chloe because I'm clearly not a part of this world you live in."

I sensed there was more and gave her a little prompt. "But?"

"But, despite me being initially nervous, Chloe was

so warm and welcoming and down-to-earth. She made tonight easier than I expected and made me feel…accepted, despite learning I worked as a bar waitress."

I had a feeling I knew who Stevie was silently comparing Chloe to. "Not everyone is like Alyssa," I said, giving her leg a gentle squeeze. "And Chloe, well, she might come from a very wealthy family, but there is nothing pretentious about her. She's always been incredibly kind and thoughtful."

"You're right," she said, smiling. "She was great and I felt very comfortable with her."

"Here's the thing," I said, wanting to impart some advice I hoped she took to heart, instead of feeling like she didn't belong in what she referred to as *my world*, when to *me* she fit perfectly. "You can't control how other people expect you to be, and when you're with the *right* people, you don't need to change who you are to fit in. The others can go fuck themselves. Don't change for anyone." Taking her hand, I lifted it to my mouth, kissing the back of it. "You're more than enough, just as you are."

"Thank you," she said softly, just as Dylan turned into the drop-off area of The Cortland. "I appreciate that."

We got out of the car and once we were in the elevator heading up to my apartment, Stevie pulled her phone from her purse and began texting someone.

"If you're messaging Valerie, tell her you're staying the night at my place," I said.

"Bossy much?" Stevie said, a wry grin on her lips. "I might be joining you for a 'nightcap' of sorts, but I have work tomorrow morning."

"So do I." She opened her mouth to reply, but I didn't give her the chance. I flashed her a wicked grin. "Don't worry, I'll wake you up in plenty of time to get ready for the office because I plan to fuck you good and hard before you go. I want you nice and sore so you'll think of me when you feel that ache throughout the day."

"You are so depraved," she said, but the desire in her eyes told me that she had no issues with that scenario.

"Guilty as charged," I replied unapologetically as the doors opened to my penthouse. "You have no idea how difficult it's been keeping my hands off you this past week and a half. A hand job in the shower while thinking about our one night together is a poor substitute for how good your pussy feels clenching around my cock. That's the last thing I want to re-member before I head off to the office in the morning."

"I have an idea of how hard it's been," she coun-tered, following me through the entryway and into the main area, where the living room light automatically switched on as we walked in. "Trust me, you aren't the only one who replayed our night together in their mind while getting off. My vibrator doesn't come close to comparing to your fingers and cock."

"And my mouth," I teased, shrugging out of my

jacket and laying it over the back of the sofa before removing my tie, enjoying our playful banter. "Don't forget how many orgasms it was responsible for."

Her husky laughter felt like a direct stroke along my dick. "Yeah. That very, *very* talented mouth. And tongue."

She turned toward me, and looking directly into my eyes, she slowly, seductively, reached up and removed the pins from her updo, until all that silky hair cascaded down around her shoulders—clearly inviting me to act on the promise I'd made earlier, of gripping those strands in my fist as I fucked her.

But this temptress wasn't done making my cock hard as stone, because she retrieved her lipstick from her purse and outlined her fuckable mouth with a fresh coat of red. Her eyes shimmered with a *come and get me* dare, and I didn't even hesitate to close the distance between us and hoist her over my shoulder like a goddamn caveman.

She shrieked in surprise as I strode to my bedroom, the sound mingling with her laughter, and when she tried to squirm and kick her feet, I smacked her ass with my free hand, knowing the firm swat had to have stung by her quick inhale of breath.

I caressed my palm over the spot, already feeling the warmth from her skin radiating through the thin fabric of her dress. "Just for the record, you might have thought you had the upper hand out in the living room by that little act—" Which, for a moment, she had. "—but you're not the one in charge tonight. Got it?"

"Yes, *sir*," she said breathlessly, using words she knew would inflame me even more.

Reaching my room, I set her on her feet, giving her a moment to steady herself on her heels before I issued my next order. "Take off your dress."

While I unbuttoned my shirt and shrugged out of it, then removed my shoes and socks, I watched her unzip her dress and with a little shimmy, it fell to the floor and she kicked it aside.

I groaned at the black lace lingerie she wore and how sexy it looked against her creamy skin, but there was something I wanted more. "Get rid of the bra, too," I said gruffly. "I want to see your gorgeous tits."

She obeyed without hesitation, my blood running so hot at seeing those perfect breasts and tight nipples on display that I wanted to pinch and bite and suck. She took a step toward me, but I quickly shook my head to stop her.

"You know what I want, Stevie," I murmured as I unbuckled my belt and unzipped my slacks over the thickest, hardest erection I'd had in recent memory. "Get on your knees like a good girl."

I honestly expected a little pushback, a bit of impudence, so her eager acquiescence surprised *and* delighted me. She knelt in front of me, her eyes hooded and licking those red lips in anticipation as she watched me push my pants and boxer briefs down until they dropped to my ankles and I could step out of them.

My cock was so stiff it stood at attention against

my stomach, and with a sinful gleam in her eye she leaned forward and licked the underside of my shaft, all the way to the crown. My stomach muscles tightened as her tongue swirled around the head then traced the slit, lapping up the drop of pre-come already gathering there.

A low growl rumbled in my chest as she teased my cock, and the little smirk she gave me as she cast her eyes upward to mine told me she was deliberately keeping me on edge.

I was dying to feel the wet heat of her mouth surrounding my cock, to see that red lipstick make its mark along my shaft. I raked my hand through Stevie's hair, then twisted my fingers tight around those long, blonde strands so that she couldn't move her head, unless I let her. And right now, she was mine to command, and she didn't seem to mind the power dynamic one bit.

I gripped my dick in my free hand and tapped the head against her scarlet lips. "Open up. I want that pretty mouth of yours wrapped around my cock."

My demand was thick with lust as she parted her lips and I pressed forward, feeling the silky, wet caress of her tongue along every inch until I had as much as I could of my shaft enveloped in her mouth. When I withdrew, she sucked, and I hissed out a breath, losing myself in pure, decadent sensation.

As I thrust in and out, slow and deep, she trailed her nails up along my outer thighs, that scrape of pain escalating the pleasure. I tipped my head back on a guttural groan, my entire body shuddering in warning. I was about two pumps away from coming, and while she gave no indication that she'd pull away, as fantastic as her mouth felt I wanted to come inside of her pussy more.

I pulled out of her mouth, almost changing my mind when I saw those red lipstick streaks on my cock and her swollen lips from being fucked. She looked up at me questioningly, her face beautifully flushed and her eyes glazed over with desire.

"Get up on the bed," I said, reaching beneath her arms to help her stand.

She crawled up onto the mattress, settling against the pillows as I retrieved a condom and quickly sheathed my cock. I moved up onto the bed to join her, and the first thing I did was strip off her panties, which were already soaked through. She shamelessly parted her legs for me, knees raised, giving me an unobstructed view of her glistening pussy.

I settled in between, and she inhaled sharply as I dragged the tips of my fingers between her drenched folds. "Jesus," I murmured, pushing two fingers deep inside her body and groaning at how her internal muscles clenched around those digits. "Look at how wet sucking my cock made you."

She whimpered and writhed impatiently beneath me, her fingers skimming down her stomach, and lower, to get herself off, which I wasn't about to allow. Before she could touch herself, I was there first, my mouth on her clit, my tongue circling and pressing while I fucked her with my fingers.

She made inarticulate sounds in the back of her throat, her hand sifting through my hair and gripping the strands as her hips undulated against my mouth. Normally, I'd take my time and prolong the release, but not tonight. I pushed her over the edge because I was desperate to get inside of her, to feel those residual spasms from her orgasm pulse around my cock.

I rubbed the tips of my fingers along that sweet spot just inside her channel, and with a gasp she came, her sweet moans filling my bedroom. Before she could spiral back down from her climax, I was up and over her, and she cried out as I slammed into her, all the way to the hilt.

"Grab onto the headboard and brace yourself," I told her, resisting the urge to rut like a beast inside of her until she was ready. "This is going to be a hard, fast, deep ride." Going slow wasn't an option. I needed her too badly.

She lifted her arms above her head, gripping the slats, and once I knew she was ready, I let go and went wild. I buried my hands in her hair, fusing our lips in a hot, provocative, tongue-tangling kiss. The sheer force of my thrusts, the depth and friction of my cock pistoning inside of her, left no room for anything but the enormity of the orgasm crashing through me...and the realization that I wanted so much more with this woman than just stolen moments.

I collapsed on top of her, every last bit of energy drained from me. Once my breathing slowed, I rolled off of her and made a quick trip to the bathroom. I returned a few minutes later and found her already under the covers, a soft, replete smile on her lips. Joining her, I pulled her into my arms. She cuddled against my side, her head resting on my chest and her arm draped across my body. She exhaled a soft sigh as I gently threaded my fingers through her hair.

This felt so perfect, so right, and I made a quick decision. "When Owen isn't here, I want you in my bed at night."

She lifted her head and arched a brow at me. "Is that an order?"

Now that we were no longer playing sexy bedroom games, I knew *this* independent, self-sufficient woman would bristle at me making demands. I also didn't think she was ready to hear that my feelings for her were evolving much quicker than I'd ever anticipated, and it wasn't all completely about sex, but just…being with her and enjoying her company. Our physical chemistry was just an added bonus.

As well as tonight's dinner had gone, I was still aware of Stevie's insecurities when it came to fitting into my life. To her, this was all a temporary arrangement with benefits, a fake relationship designed to keep my ex-wife from using what she perceived as leverage against me in our custody battle for Owen.

As much as I was ready to discuss my developing feelings, I didn't think Stevie was ready to accept and believe that what I wanted with her was something far more real. So I had to settle for the next best thing, and having her in my life, and in my bed, on a regular basis, was a start.

"No, it's not an order," I murmured. "It's a request. I enjoy spending time with you, and you can't deny that the sex is pretty damn fantastic." Yeah, I'd use that to my advantage if I had to.

She lightly, playfully, scratched her nails along my abdomen. "You're awfully sure of yourself."

I rolled her onto her back, my body half draped across hers. Holding her gaze, I cupped one of her breasts in my hand and tweaked her nipple, making her gasp in surprise. "Do I need to prove, once again, how good we are in bed together?"

Her eyes darkened with renewed desire as I trailed my fingers down her stomach and stroked them between her thighs. "You might have to."

So, I did, dipping my head to latch onto one of her stiff nipples while my fingers plied her pussy and clit and brought her to another orgasm that had her shaking, moaning, then eventually sighing with satisfaction.

I grinned down at her flushed face. "Is that a yes?"

A teasing light flickered in her eyes. "Do you think I'm that easy?"

I chuckled. "Never, and I love how you keep me guessing," I said, then grew more serious. "But right now, I just want to know that I can enjoy you in the evenings when Owen isn't here. That I have something to look forward to at the end of a long work day. However, if you need more persuasion of why you should agree, I'm up for the challenge."

"You most certainly are," she said, her hand wrapping around my erection and giving it a playful stroke. "And I'm thinking I need more persuasion, please."

By the time I was done with her, the only word she could utter was *yes*, and knowing she'd be spending a helluva lot more time in my bed, and in my life, was all that mattered to me.

CHAPTER THIRTEEN

Stevie

I WAITED IN the valet area at The Cortland for Raven to arrive in the rideshare she'd ordered to pick me up. We were going shopping to find dresses for the upcoming Inspired by Art Charity Gala we were both attending with our men that upcoming weekend. As soon as the light blue sedan pulled up to the curb and I saw my friend sitting inside, I joined her in the back seat and the driver merged his way back into early mid-morning Wednesday traffic.

"What are you smiling about?" Raven asked.

Her question made me realize that I *was* walking around with a perma-grin these days, but I kept my reply all about her. "I'm spending the day with my best friend and that makes me happy."

"And maybe Caleb does, too?" she ventured to ask.

I shrugged without a verbal response, because despite my agreement with Caleb that was going on four weeks now, our arrangement still felt very...complicated. Or at least my feelings for the man did. Because every day with him made me fall a little harder for him, a little deeper. And I wasn't sure what to do about those feelings that never should have been part of the fake relationship equation to begin with. Despite being happy in the moment, I couldn't help but consider the future and the potential heartache I was probably going to endure once the custody case for Owen was finalized and we went our separate ways.

"So, sleeping in Caleb's bed every night when Owen isn't there doesn't make you happy?" Raven persisted. "Even a little bit?"

Yeah, I regretted telling her about that agreement I'd made with Caleb, because Raven saw it as something deeper and more intimate than two people enjoying great sex—even if I did secretly wish that everything about our relationship was real. But even then, I had those deep-seated insecurities and voices of doubt in my head that reminded me we came from two vastly different socioeconomic backgrounds, and fitting into Caleb's life beyond this deal we'd made was unlikely.

I met Raven's gaze, keeping my tone kind, but firm. "I know you're trying to matchmake, but you need to stop trying to make this arrangement with Caleb into something more than it is." I added a smile to soften my words, because I knew she meant well. "Is it convenient having a guy with benefits in this world where there are so many creeps on dating apps? Yes. So, I'm enjoying the time we're spending together, and let's leave it at that, okay?"

"Okay," she said, and I could see by the look in her eyes that she wasn't offended by my response, which was one of the things I loved about Raven. Her ability to be open and honest, yet also understand when I needed her to back down.

The truth was, I was starting to feel *too* intertwined in Caleb's life, and it was a scary feeling knowing there was an end date. When Owen was with Alyssa, I spent those nights in Caleb's bed. We had dinner together, we watched shows that we both enjoyed with me cuddled against him on the couch, and we discussed our days like an actual couple in a way that felt too real and domesticated.

And when Caleb had Owen, I spent those evenings having dinner with them both, which I loved because Owen was such a great kid. I still had time to study during my days off, and I had two finals coming up that would wrap up all my coursework for my degree. So, I was trying to keep focused on that, along with finding another suitable and affordable apartment for Valerie and me to move into once my obligation to Caleb was over, rather than obsessing over what my life was going to be like in about a month, without Caleb and Owen in it.

"So, give me the update on Valerie and her job at Dare PR," Raven said, breaking into my thoughts. "And, most importantly, this Jack guy you said is interested in her."

I appreciated the change in subject. "She's doing great, as I knew she would. And Jack…well, he knows she recently came out of a bad relationship, so they're taking it slow. Some days, they meet for a coffee in the morning before work, and occasionally they have lunch together. She seems to really like him, too."

I was thrilled for Valerie. That she was trying to move on and she had someone like Jack who was willing to go slow and keep things casual until she was ready for more.

"So, things have been quiet on the Mark front?" Raven ventured to ask, since I'd told her about the call he'd made to Valerie's cell from a burner number.

"Yes. For now."

She tipped her head curiously. "What do you mean, for now?"

I sighed. "Call me pessimistic, but abusive, controlling men like Mark don't just go away, and him being quiet unnerves me. I'm…cautiously optimistic, but having lived with a father with those same tendencies makes me wary. It's crazy to me that Mark's family is so wealthy, yet they let him get away with this disturbing behavior. It's like he thinks he's untouchable *because* of that wealth."

Raven nodded in understanding. "Just like Cassandra never held Lance accountable for his actions. Some people just think they're entitled. And yes, that's scary because they believe consequences don't apply to them."

I agreed. "For now, we're secure in the apartment that Caleb has us staying in, and I'm already looking into places that have a doorman and security for when we move out." I was grateful to Caleb that my sister and I wouldn't have to move back to our old neighborhood.

The car slowed in the heavy traffic and tried to merge over to drop us off at the curb. I glanced out the back seat window, frowning when I realized what part of Manhattan we were in. One that was upscale with rows upon rows of exclusive, high-end designer shops.

"You said you knew a place where we could buy dresses for the charity gala," I said, looking back at Raven. "Anything located on Fifth Avenue is way beyond my budget."

Raven flashed me a gregarious grin. "Just humor me, okay? We're going to a boutique that carries more formal dresses, and I want your opinion on what to choose."

I relaxed at her explanation. I could help Raven select a gown at one of these ritzy places, and then we'd hit up a more affordable department store for me. Despite the money I had sitting in my bank account thanks to Caleb's generosity, the last thing I wanted to do was squander thousands of dollars on a dress I'd only wear once.

The driver finally found an open spot to let us out, and I met up with Raven on the sidewalk. She looped her arm through mine, leading me past Christian Dior, Louis Vuitton, and even Bergdorf Goodman until we reached a store that might have been smaller than those other designers, but the moment we walked in it gave off that same exclusive, elite atmosphere.

Raven, God love her, walked in like she owned the joint, even though she was wearing a casual blouse and well-worn jeans like I was. Then again, she *had* come from money, even if she was estranged from her adoptive mother and hadn't relied on the Kanes' family wealth in a very long time. But she'd also married a man with copious amounts of money…so, yeah, she was far more used to this kind of shopping experience than I was.

There were two salesladies in the store. One was checking out a customer at the register, and the other was helping another shopper choose a pair of heels in the shoe section. Both women eyed Raven and I with distaste the moment we entered, as if we were two homeless people who'd wandered in off the street.

Feeling out of place and uncomfortable, I stayed close to Raven's side as she browsed the front area of the store, seemingly oblivious to the other women's stares—or more like she didn't give a shit what they thought of her—while I didn't dare touch a thing as she continued to peruse a section with a few gorgeous gowns and dresses. The one thing I noticed was that there was no indication on any of the garments of what they cost.

I stood next to Raven, speaking in a low tone. "These gowns don't have prices on them."

Raven smirked at me. "Of course they don't, because money is no object to the women who shop here."

CARLY PHILLIPS & ERIKA WILDE

Yeah, that definitely excluded me.

"Can I help the two of you with something?"

The snobby voice from directly behind us made me stiffen, and when both Raven and I turned around, the saleslady's mouth was flattened with disdain as her gaze flicked down the length of us, clearly disapproving of our attire. Probably of us in general.

"Yes, you absolutely can," Raven said in a bright, animated tone. "We'd like to try on a few gowns."

We? I had to clench my jaw because my immediate response was to blurt out no, I most definitely did *not* want to try on dresses here, because *what the hell, Raven?*

The woman gave us another disapproving look that made my stomach churn. "Can I ask how you'll be paying for any purchases today?" she asked, still in that haughty tone. "We have a no shopping without intention policy and we require pre-approval before pulling the gowns for you to try on."

A rule meant to exclude casual browsers, no doubt.

"Of course." Smiling sweetly, Raven opened her purse and withdrew her form of payment from her wallet. "Here's my credit card," she said, handing over the sleek black card before retrieving a second one and giving that to the saleslady, as well. "And this one is for her," she said, indicating me.

I stood there in confusion as the woman pursed her lips, her gaze narrowed on the last card Raven had given her before her eyes raised back up again. "The name on this card says Caleb Kane. His wife, Alyssa Kane, is a client here but she has her own card. I'm sure this has to be some kind of mistake," she said, as if Raven had found the credit card laying on the sidewalk and was trying to pass it off as her own.

"No, not a mistake at all," Raven replied pleasantly, giving no indication that the woman had deliberately insulted her. "Oh, and for the record, Alyssa is Caleb's *ex*-wife. Call the credit card company and you can verify that he's added Stevie Palmer as an authorized user to the account, unlimited credit."

I refrained, just barely, from letting my jaw drop open in shock.

The woman lifted her chin in an imposing manner. "I most certainly *will* do that."

The saleslady walked away, and Raven just rolled her eyes at the woman's condescending attitude while my mind was spinning, trying to make sense of what had just happened.

I shook my head. "What is going on, and why and how am I an authorized user on Caleb's *black* credit card?"

Raven shrugged. "After you mentioned to Caleb last week that we were going shopping for gowns today for the gala, he came by The Back Door and gave me his credit card to use to buy you whatever you want."

I narrowed my gaze at her, because now standing in this boutique seemed calculated and planned. "But why are we *here*, specifically?" I asked, when there were many other name brand designer stores on Fifth Avenue. "In what is probably one of the most exclusive, expensive boutiques in Manhattan."

"We're here to buy gowns for the gala, of course," she said flippantly, and then she grinned, her eyes lighting up with wicked glee. "And for funsies, to yank Alyssa's chain because you *know* that woman is going to call her first thing after we leave and tell her that Caleb gave you carte blanche in this store that *she* frequents, which is a nice little way to solidify to her that you're his girlfriend."

"You are diabolical," I said, in the most loving tone possible. "But I can't just spend Caleb's money so frivolously."

Raven sighed and gave me a pointed look. "He knew you'd feel this way and he told me to tell you that since he asked you to accompany him to the gala, and it's a formal event, this is on him. Whatever you want and whatever *I* deem necessary for you, as well. He said not to take no for an answer."

"This is crazy," I said, still having a difficult time accepting his generosity.

This time, Raven exhaled an exasperated breath. "For God's sake, Stevie. Caleb has more money than he knows what to do with and you're *not* taking advantage of him," she said, reading my mind. "If he wants to spoil you, then let him and enjoy the experience, which will in turn make him happy. And, if you feel so inclined, I'm sure you can find a few creative ways to thank him later." She gave me a saucy wink.

I forced myself to relax, to push aside my own pride and allow myself to embrace Caleb's generosity.

Easier said than done, but I also understood that in order to fit in with the upper class at the charity event, I did need to look the part.

When the saleslady returned a short while later, her whole attitude had changed from disdain to hospitable and friendly. Clearly everything had been pre-approved without any issues, and now seeing us as a nice fat commission, we were given the white-glove treatment.

Whatever dresses we wanted were pulled in our sizes as we drank flutes of champagne and smirked behind the woman's back at her eager-to-please behavior. We were shown the boutique's exclusive collections and limited edition gowns that were kept in the back for only those clients who met the monetary criteria. Once we had a plethora to choose from, we were ushered into a private, elegant changing area with a dais and multiple mirrors. As we spent the next few hours trying on the dresses, I couldn't help but be amused at the way Raven deliberately ran the saleslady ragged with random requests, always asked in the sweetest, most polite manner.

Whenever the woman rushed out of the room to do Raven's bidding—to bring her a pair of matching shoes, or other accessories that Raven then decided didn't work for her—I saw the devious twinkle in her eye and the two of us giggled, the amount of champagne we consumed contributing to our silly moods.

After trying on nearly a dozen gowns, I finally found "the one". I knew it the moment I stepped up on the dais and saw my reflection in the red, strapless, formfitting gown, and Raven's gasp confirmed it. A short while later, Raven found hers, a one-shoulder style in a stunning amethyst hue.

Raven insisted we buy a new pair of heels to go with the dresses, along with appropriate earrings and formal handbags to complete the look. When we were done and the saleslady rang up our purchases, my stomach was in knots awaiting the total. Except I quickly learned in places like this, they didn't give you a final amount. They just ran the credit card because cost was not an issue to their clients, or a customer carrying a no preset limit Centurion card.

We left the boutique and went to lunch, both of us ravenous after a morning of trying on gowns. Then, Raven surprised me with another stop at a trendy hair salon in the city, where she'd made both of us appointments. A few hours later, my blonde hair was brightened with highlights, as was Raven's. It had been years since I'd treated myself to a good trim and long layers, and by the time we walked out of the salon, my silky hair styled into soft waves, I literally felt like a million bucks.

Caleb's jaw-dropping reaction when I arrived at his penthouse for dinner later that evening shored up my confidence, as well. Even though my first instinct was to tell him "you shouldn't have", I thanked him for the day he'd given me without any qualifiers, letting him know how much I appreciated his thoughtful gesture.

I could tell my acceptance made him happy as he framed my face in his hands and stared into my eyes.

"You deserve beautiful things, and I'm glad I can give them to you."

His husky tone and genuine words made me melt and feel as though I was living in a fairy tale, where he was Prince Charming and I was Cinderella. It was a romantic, whimsical notion, and one I told myself not to get used to, because beneath the makeover and gorgeous things he'd bought me today, I was still the girl who'd grown up in a trailer park and Caleb Kane was still out of my league.

WHEN I WALKED into the conference room at work the next morning for a team meeting for PureGlow, arriving before any of my other coworkers besides Jack, he did a double take at my new hair style and I laughed at his wide-eyed shock.

"Damn, you look…great," he said, his tone amazed.

I set my laptop and paper cup of coffee down on the table and grinned at him. "So, are you insinuating that I don't look great every day?" I teased.

"Ahh, shit. I walked right into that trap, didn't I?" he said, and grimaced. "You always look good—"

"Thank you for the compliment," I said, letting him off the hook so he didn't have to fumble for an explanation, and he looked relieved. "How was coffee with Valerie this morning?"

Usually, the two of us took the subway to the office together when I worked on Tuesdays and Thursdays, but since starting at Dare PR almost three weeks ago, a few times a week Valerie left a bit earlier to meet Jack at a nearby café for coffee before work started.

On those days, she took an Uber, and admittedly, it made me nervous knowing she was out on her own without me around because of Mark, but there had been nothing since that phone call and I knew I had to let go of my own fears for her and let her live her life without me hovering.

"So, I held her hand on the very short walk to the office after our coffee date," Jack said, grinning at that small step forward in their friendship. "I told her I wanted to take her on a proper date, and she said yes. So, we're going out on Saturday."

I crossed my arms over my chest and arched a brow at him. "What do you consider a proper date?"

He laughed at my inquisition. "I was thinking dinner, and a show."

I nodded, impressed. "Okay, I approve."

"You approve?" Amused, he tipped his head at me. "Isn't Valerie older than you?"

I took a drink of my warm coffee and shrugged. "She is, but that doesn't mean I can't be protective of her."

The humor on his face gave way to seriousness. "I'd never intentionally hurt her," he said, which I believed. "I like her. A lot."

"Spoiler alert," I said, grinning at him. "If you don't already know, the feeling is mutual."

A low, warm chuckle escaped him. "I kind of suspected that when she let me hold her hand."

I laughed, too, genuinely happy for my sister as I checked the time on my cellphone. It was ten minutes later than the time Jack had set for the meeting, and it was just still the two of us. "Where is everyone else?" I asked.

"I called off the meeting."

"You did?" I asked, surprised that I hadn't gotten the memo, too. Especially when I had so many more great ideas to share with everyone on the PureGlow campaign. "Why?"

He looked me in the eye, his expression unreadable. "Because Brandy and Samantha asked me to send you to their office instead."

I wasn't sure what to make of that, but it sounded serious enough that my stomach churned with unease because I'd never been *sent* to their office before. To meet with the two of them, no less.

"Oh. Okay."

I gathered up my laptop and other things and headed out of the conference room, my mind whirring with possible reasons for this random meeting, none of them great. I was an intern—a paid one, yes, but the truth was, they had no obligation to me whatsoever. I'd been hired on to gain practical experience in a marketing firm two days a week, and as much as I loved working at Dare PR—and even though they'd discussed bringing me in on a full-time basis once I had my degree—well, it didn't bode well that I was having this meeting *before* I'd achieved that goal.

I walked down the hall to the executive wing, seeing through the glass wall that both Brandy and Samantha were in Samantha's office. They were standing together inside, talking, and I couldn't get a read on their moods.

"Hey, Stevie," my sister said, greeting me from her desk in front of Brandy's office where she handled all the assistant duties for her boss. "Brandy and Samantha are waiting for you and said for you to head inside when you arrived."

I searched my sister's expression to see if she knew what I was walking into, but she was all bright-eyed, happy smile enthusiasm these days, giving me no clue whatsoever.

I set my laptop on the corner of Valerie's desk and walked into my boss's office. "Good morning, Samantha, Brandy," I said.

They both gave me smiles and returned the greeting, then Samantha rounded her desk to take the chair behind it. "Have a seat," she said, waving toward the two chairs in front of her desk.

I settled into one, and Brandy took the other. Feeling nervous, I clasped my hands in my lap.

"I guess I'll just get right down to business," Samantha said, meeting my gaze. "We're going to have to cut your two days a week."

I tried not to flinch or react to the news, but damn that felt like a sucker punch to the stomach. "Do you mind me asking why?" I glanced from Samantha to

Brandy.

Brandy grinned. "Because we're offering you a full-time position here at Dare PR, starting as soon as possible."

Confusion rippled through me. "I...I don't understand."

Samantha grimaced, seemingly realizing where my mind had gone. "We wanted to surprise you, but I can see that plan kind of backfired and you were expecting the worst. But, well...surprise!"

All my anxiety faded away, and excitement settled in its place as I tried to catch up. "But I haven't finished my final classes yet. I don't have my degree." I still had about a month to go to wrap up all my coursework.

"Your degree is just a formality," Brandy said, grinning. "Even without it we'd still make you this same offer. You've proven yourself more than capable."

Samantha nodded in agreement. "PureGlow has been so impressed with your campaign ideas and they requested that *you* head up the account. After discussing things with Jack, who is one of your biggest advocates, by the way, we're promoting you to a full-time position as a marketing strategist. You'll be working directly beneath Jack and reporting to him since he's a senior manager, but we need you to start full-time as soon as possible. Like, next week. Is that something you can do?"

My head spun as I tried to process everything. Accepting the position meant resigning from The Back Door permanently, but Raven had already assured me that she was covering my shifts just fine. I knew she'd understand, because this had been my end goal, anyway. It had just happened faster than I'd anticipated.

"Yes," I said enthusiastically. "Yes, I can do that."

The two of them presented me with an impressive salary that came with health insurance and benefits, a retirement plan, stock options, and bonuses. By the time I walked out of their office I was floating on a cloud, grateful that my dedication to Dare PR, and all my hard work, was starting to pay off.

CHAPTER FOURTEEN

Stevie

THE ENTIRE WEEK had passed in an overwhelming rush of activity. Between my day with Raven on Wednesday, my promotion at work on Thursday, and Caleb insisting on properly celebrating my first real career achievement on Friday—which had included an insanely expensive bottle of champagne, a bouquet of two dozen roses, and dinner at a five-star restaurant—it had been a whirlwind of events.

Today, Saturday, was the Inspired by Art Charity Gala. I'd spent the morning and afternoon with Valerie, doing our normal Saturday laundry and grocery shopping routine, and enjoying a session at the yoga studio in the building. Afterward, she'd helped me with my hair and makeup, had zipped me into my gorgeous, fitted, strapless red gown for the event, and then Jack had arrived to pick her up for their first real date night together.

She'd been so giddy it had been adorable. I, of course, couldn't help but tease Jack about being a gentleman and getting my sister home at a respectable time, and he took it all in stride. I made Valerie promise to text me later so I knew what her plans were since I'd be spending the night with Caleb. I just needed to know whether she'd be at home or at Jack's so I didn't worry.

A short while later, Caleb arrived at the apartment, and as soon as I opened the door we both stared at one another in awe. I couldn't tear my eyes off him because he was wearing a fitted black tuxedo and looked sexy as hell, and he smelled amazing wearing that expensive cologne I loved that made my sex clench whenever I got a whiff of it...like now.

But it was the reverent way that Caleb looked at me, his expression filled with so much appreciation and adoration that those emotions made my breath catch. I'd never felt so beautiful in my entire life. So confident that tonight, in a room filled with his peers, I was going to make him proud to have me on his arm.

But then those eyes of his darkened as they took in my blonde hair that Valerie had styled in glamorous waves reminiscent of a classic Hollywood starlet. His gaze retraced a path across the tempting red lipstick I wore, lingering on my mouth before dipping lower to my gown, most likely admiring the way the cut of the bodice lifted my breasts and gave me fantastic cleavage. How the waistline nipped in and the slit that exposed one leg to mid-thigh showcased the most stunning, crystal-encrusted, red strappy heels that Raven had insisted I buy. Seeing Caleb's reaction now, I was glad I'd indulged.

"*Fuck me*," he said in a low, sexy growl as he lifted his eyes back up to mine after cataloguing all the *red* encasing my body, a deliberate choice on my part. "Are you trying to make my dick permanently hard tonight?"

I laughed, secretly pleased that my ploy had worked. "Maybe."

"Wicked girl," he said huskily, a sinful smile curving his lips. "You'll pay for that later."

I grinned unrepentantly. "I certainly hope so."

I grabbed my clutch and he took my hand, escorting me down the elevator and out of the building to where Dylan was waiting to drive us to the event. We settled into the back seat, sitting side by side, with him still holding my hand, his thumb absently stroking across my knuckles.

"So, is there anything specific I need to know about tonight?" I asked once we'd merged out into traffic toward the Meridian Hotel, where this evening's event was being held.

He thought for a moment, then turned his head to look at me. "So, I already mentioned that Alyssa is going to be there. Last Sunday, when I dropped off Owen for the week, she told me she was dating an architect and he was coming as her date, not that I give a damn what she does in her personal life, so long as it doesn't adversely affect Owen."

His tone was harsh and I understood why. His concern for Owen superseded anything else. I also had a feeling she'd told him about the new man in her life, most likely to make Caleb jealous, but it was clear that he was not the least bit envious.

"She's unpredictable, as you've seen, so we'll just keep our distance," he went on. "The ballroom at the Meridian is huge, and we're seated with the Sterling family, who are all there to support Fallon. She's contributing pieces of her artwork for the auction. Since she's an artist herself, and owns a gallery down-town, she's a big advocate of art programs, grants, and community-based art projects that support emerging artists."

Having met Fallon through Raven, who was her sister-in-law, I smiled. "I'm looking forward to seeing all the art at the auction. I'm not a connoisseur by any stretch, but it's fun to see all the different styles and how each artist expresses themselves."

We arrived at the hotel a short while later and with my arm in Caleb's, we headed into the ballroom, which had been transformed into a stunning vision of elegance. Crystal chandeliers hung from the high, vaulted ceilings, while tables adorned with towering floral centerpieces and flickering candles created a warm, sophisticated ambiance. The air was filled with the soft melodies of a string quartet and everywhere I looked was a sea of tuxedos and jewel-toned ballgowns.

Yes, I was out of my element at this charity gala, but there was also something exhilarating about experiencing this once-in-a-lifetime—*for me*—occasion, and I soaked it all in, enjoying everything about the breathtaking glamour and grandeur of the venue.

We met up with Remy and Raven and spent the next hour mingling with other guests while I sipped on champagne and Caleb opted for a Dirty Dare scotch, neat. Raven and I chatted with Chloe while the men talked, and Samantha was there since she was married to Fallon's brother, Dex.

I couldn't deny that it felt amazing being on Caleb's arm, how he introduced me to people I didn't know and how they automatically accepted me because of who I was with—a man with wealth and power, who exuded such an undeniable magnetism it was difficult not to be drawn to him.

Never once did I feel self-conscious. I didn't feel like an imposter. I felt like I belonged, and for tonight, I wholeheartedly embraced the feeling.

At the end of the cocktail hour, I glanced over at Raven and saw her looking at something, or someone, outside of our group, her eyes narrowed enough to make me curious to follow her line of vision straight to…Alyssa, who was surrounded by two other couples. The man standing next to her, whom she had her arm looped through his was a good-looking man in his mid-forties—her prestigious architect date, no doubt.

Of course I'd known it was only a matter of time before I saw her, and it was clear by the way she was speaking to other women, and how they glanced our way and laughed, that she was probably talking about me.

"She's such a bitch," Raven said, a little heat in her

tone.

I glanced back at my friend, seeing her pursed lips and the glare she cast Alyssa's way—looking like an adorable, protective little pit bull terrier on my behalf.

"As long as she keeps her distance, I'm fine," I said, and I truly, surprisingly, meant that. I wasn't going to let a few catty women ruin my evening with Caleb, at such a spectacular event.

Raven met my gaze, her eyes flashing a little fire. "If she stirs up any trouble for you, I have no issues kicking her ass."

I laughed. "Oh, yeah, I'm sure that would go over *really* well at an event like this, but thank you. It's the thought that counts."

Raven smirked. "She's probably beyond jealous that you look fucking fantastic in that one-of-a-kind gown that she knows Caleb bought for you."

Before I could reply, I felt Caleb's arm around my waist as he pulled me close to his side in a delightfully assertive manner for anyone to see. Then, he surprised me further by brushing his lips across my cheek. "Raven is right, you know," he murmured against my ear, establishing more intimacy between us. "You *do* look fucking fantastic."

His words thrilled me. I didn't even care if the sweet kiss and his possessive actions were for show. Tonight, I let myself pretend it was all real.

Dinner was announced, a five-course meal followed by a few speeches from various benefactors in the art world, thanking guests for their generous donations and encouraging them to support the program further by bidding on the artwork at the silent auction.

Caleb and I headed in that direction, while the string quartet switched out for more lively dance music. We strolled through the area, taking in all the pieces of different artwork, from classic and modern paintings to elaborate sculptures to photorealism and more, discussing some of the offerings along the way. I found myself fascinated by all the various aesthetics and styles, but the one piece I was drawn to the most was Fallon's bright and colorful pop art.

I stopped Caleb in front of her large, framed painting with colorful hearts around the word LOVE that seemed to leap off the canvas in a three-dimensional technique. I glanced at the piece of paper on the table in front of Fallon's artwork. The bid was already up over seventy thousand, a drop in the bucket for any of these wealthy guests in attendance, but at least it was all going to a good cause.

Caleb studied the piece for a moment, head tilted to the side, before saying, "That's quite…loud."

I laughed at what he deemed a polite description. I knew it was nothing against Fallon, personally, but Caleb's tastes were much more…refined.

"It's funky and fun and very cool," I corrected him, because while I could appreciate all the other artwork in the room, to me they were boring in comparison, not that I'd say that out loud. "*This* makes me smile."

"Well, I do love your smile," he said, clearly trying to find a positive to the conversation.

I rolled my eyes at him. "Seriously, though, this is a piece that would draw everyone's attention and start a conversation," I said, before I decided to tease him a bit. "This artwork would look amazing in your living room. All those splashes of color would break up that monotonous, manly, navy décor and make things more interesting."

The way he grimaced spoke for him. No way was he trading in his clean, streamlined aesthetic for something so quirky and fun.

We left the silent auction and returned to the main ballroom. We continued to visit with people he knew, and a few I was acquainted with, as well, while others enjoyed the upbeat music and danced. When a slow tune came on and the lights dimmed, it was Caleb who surprised me by leading me out onto the dance floor and pulling me into his arms.

I was keenly aware that Alyssa was also there with her date, far enough away that we wouldn't run into them, but close enough for me to feel her eyes on me, which I'd noticed throughout most of the evening.

Ignoring her, I smiled up at Caleb, focusing my attention solely on him. "Look at you, taking the initiative to dance. I didn't even have to twist your arm to get you out here."

"I'll admit, I had ulterior motives," he said, tucking the hand he was holding against his chest, making our connection look and feel even more intimate. "I've hit my limit of socializing and *this* is the view I've been really wanting all night long."

He made his point by letting his eyes flicker down to my lips, then lowering to my breasts, which had been plumped up, the upper swells spilling over the top of my gown since they were pressed against his chest.

I laughed lightly. "You're such a predictable man."

A wicked grin tipped up the corners of his mouth. "If lusting after you makes me predictable, so be it."

We continued to sway to the slow, romantic song, and I laid my cheek against his shoulder, relaxing against him. Closing my eyes, I inhaled his arousing cologne, now mingled with the scent of his warm skin. I didn't care who was watching as I basked in Caleb's attention. It was a magical night I wouldn't forget anytime soon.

As the last notes indicated the end to the song, I glanced back up at his face, recognizing the heat and hunger in his eyes. The way he held me so close, the press of his hard, strong body along the length of mine, narrowed everything down to just him and me in that moment.

"You ready to head home?" he asked in a low, husky voice.

That tone made me shiver, because I knew it was every indication of what awaited me once we arrived back at his place. His hands and mouth on my body, the kind of orgasms that were bone-deep satisfying, and him filling me up in ways that went beyond sex.

"I am," I said, and nodded, already anticipating the second part of the night. "I just need to use the ladies' room, and I'll be good to go."

Taking my hand, he walked me there, then released his hold. "I'll be waiting over there for you," he said, nodding to a spot a short distance away.

I walked into the lounge area, startled to see Alyssa there by herself, standing at one of the vanities, her back to me. I came to an abrupt stop. I'd had no idea she'd be in here or else I never would have put myself in a position of being alone with her.

But it was too late, and hearing me enter, she glanced up into the mirror in front of her, seeing me behind her in the reflection. Clearly just as startled by my appearance, her hands flinched, and the pills she'd been pouring into her palm from a prescription bottle scattered across the counter.

"Fuck," she whispered in a panic, then more angrily, "*fuck*."

I watched her scramble to retrieve the white oval-shaped pills, her movements clumsy and her fingers not quite able to grasp the tablets. "Are you okay?" I asked, unable to ignore the situation.

"Oh, yeah, I'm fucking fine," she snapped, her words a bit slurred as she managed to get the rest of the pills back into the bottle but struggled with putting the cap back on. "And do you really give a shit?"

It was obvious that she was either intoxicated by alcohol or high from pills, or both. And the thing was, if she was struggling with her sobriety, I *did* care, for

Owen's sake. But it wasn't my place to express my concern, or question her, or anything else. However, it was something I knew I'd have to tell Caleb so he was aware of the situation.

Not wanting to engage with her, I started to walk past her to the restrooms, but she whirled around, stepping just enough into my path to make me abruptly stop or crash into her.

Her gaze flicked down the length of me, and not in a complimentary way. "I have to say, Caleb's money went a long way in making you look like you belong in our world, but let's be honest. Trailer park trash like you will never fit in," she said, her words spoken slowly because of her intoxication, but they were no less cruel. "You can make yourself look pretty on the outside, but you can never erase how ugly your past is, and where you come from."

Everything inside of me went stone cold at her insinuation, but before I could formulate a response, she continued.

"Does Caleb know that you were raised in a trailer park?" she asked, her lips curling up in an unflattering sneer. "That your father murdered your mother and is rotting in prison because of it?"

My stomach churned, because I realized that Caleb had been completely serious when he'd told me that Alyssa would probably hire a PI to check me out. It was something I hadn't thought about since our initial discussion, but here she was, gloating over what she'd discovered.

A spark of glee lit her glassy eyes. "He doesn't know, does he?"

The dread I'd been feeling must have shown on my face and I did my best to school my expression and remain cool under pressure. I'd never felt the need to tell Caleb about my painful past with my father because, honestly, the truth was mortifying and it had never factored into our *temporary* relationship. And if Alyssa thought something like this gave her leverage in the custody of Owen, her idea was flawed.

"Why does it matter?" I asked her, keeping my voice steady. "Caleb's own brother is sitting in prison, which means *my* past certainly isn't going to hurt Caleb's chances when it comes to the custody case."

"Oh, it doesn't matter in terms of the custody case," she said, looking pleased with what she'd discovered. "But once word gets out about where you come from, it's going to make you look desperate to everyone else in our circle. Like a fucking gold digger who was looking for a better life and decided a man like Caleb could give that to you."

I flinched at her words before I could catch myself, and Alyssa clearly took pleasure in that discomfort before she gave me one last triumphant look and walked out of the ladies' room.

Logically, I knew what she said wasn't true. I even knew that Caleb would never think such a thing of me, but if Alyssa spread the rumors and stirred the gossip, the last thing I'd ever want was to tarnish Caleb's reputation because of *my* past or how my upbringing could paint me as a woman who was only with Caleb for his money. I'd never want to put that kind of speculation on him.

Those knots in my stomach tightened. I had to talk to Caleb and tell him the truth before he heard about my past from someone else and was blindsided by the skeletons lurking in *my* closet.

As wonderful as the night had been up to this point, it clearly wasn't going to last.

CHAPTER FIFTEEN

Caleb

AS SOON AS I saw Alyssa exit the ladies' room with a smug look on her face shortly after Stevie went inside, my entire body tensed in reaction, my gut telling me that my ex had probably stirred up some kind of shit with Stevie.

My instincts were confirmed when Stevie came back out a few minutes later and approached me, her expression subdued. Gone was the lively, exuberant woman I'd been with all night, and in her place was someone who almost looked...defeated.

"What did Alyssa say to you?" I immediately asked.

She shook her head, the distress in her eyes unmistakable. "Please, can we just leave?"

It took every ounce of control I had to not demand answers so I could take care of whatever the problem was, but I respected her request and ushered her out of the ballroom while texting Dylan to bring the car around to pick us up.

But once we were settled in the back of the vehicle, I took her hand in mine and approached the issue once more. "Stevie, what happened with Alyssa?"

She looked at me, and the pain I saw in her eyes was like a direct hit to my heart. "I promise to tell you everything, but not here," she said in a soft tone. "Just…let's get back to your place and let me change out of this dress and get more comfortable first. Please?"

Not wanting to pressure her further, I relented for now. "Okay," I said, though that easy agreement went against every grain in my body when I was a man who preferred to face things head-on.

The rest of the drive was quiet as she stared out the passenger window, and it drove me insane the way it felt as though she was shutting me out, or maybe putting up her guard. There was a disconnect between us that I despised, and I was furious at the thought that Alyssa had done or said something to cause that divide.

When we arrived back at my place, I gave her the time and space she'd asked for while we both changed out of our formal attire. I pulled on a pair of sweat-pants and went back into the living room to wait for Stevie while she removed her makeup in the bathroom and joined me a short while later, wearing one of the casual cotton sleepshirts she'd kept here for her overnight stays.

She sat next to me on the couch, turning toward me and curling her legs beneath her. I waited for her to start the conversation, and she did so immediately.

"The first and most important thing I need to tell

you is that when I walked into the ladies' room, Alyssa was in the lounge area by herself," she said, her fingers absently pulling at the hem of her sleepshirt. "I caught her by surprise, and she was pouring prescription pills out of a bottle to take one, or a few, I don't know. She dropped them onto the counter as soon as she saw me because I startled her, and she had a hard time picking them back up and seemed under the influence of something. It could have been too much champagne, for all I know."

My stomach clenched and I swore beneath my breath. "Do you know what she was taking?"

She shook her head. "I wasn't close enough to see exactly what kind of pills they were, but it was definitely a bottle from a pharmacy. It could be nothing at all, but considering her past substance abuse, I wanted you to be aware of the situation."

I scrubbed a hand along my jaw. "Thank you for letting me know."

I wasn't sure what to do with the information Stevie had just given me, but my first reaction was to jump to my own conclusions, which weren't good ones and only based on my past with Alyssa. In reality, the pills could have been for her migraines, or even antibiotics…hell, I had no idea what Alyssa's current health history was, so I knew I had to be careful about making assumptions without proof.

Regardless, I was concerned because of Owen. I had him back for the week starting tomorrow, and while I thought about confronting Alyssa when she dropped him off, I knew if she had relapsed, she'd deny that the pills were anything more than just a prescription for a current ailment. And despite my worries, I had no right to demand she show me those bottles just to ease my conscience. We were divorced, and she didn't owe me anything just based on a hunch or speculation, and accusations, if inaccurate, would only cause more friction between us.

I had a week to figure things out and my first thought was to see if Remy, who was a skilled private investigator himself and had a law enforcement background, had any ideas on how to handle the situation. Or if there was a way to find out what her current prescriptions were. Doubtful, because of patient privacy laws, but the unease of it all sat in my stomach like a rock. I was just grateful that I would have Owen in my custody through next weekend, since we'd be at the Hamptons for his birthday.

"Something else happened between you and Alyssa," I said, addressing my next concern because it was imperative to me that I knew everything that had transpired between Stevie and my ex. Especially when it had changed Stevie's demeanor so drastically. "I saw the smug look on her face when she walked out of the ladies' room, and she wouldn't have looked that way if she hadn't felt as though she'd gotten the upper hand somehow after you caught her with the pills."

She shook her head and glanced away, but not before I saw the dismay etched across her features. Yes, there was something else, and it seemed more personal than the pill situation.

I gently touched her jaw and turned her face back toward mine, needing to know what had caused that distress. "Whatever it is, Stevie, you need to tell me," I said emphatically. Because I cared…more than she probably realized. She wasn't some random, one-time date for me that had an unfortunate run-in with my ex. No, Stevie was a woman I wanted to protect, in any way I could.

It didn't escape my notice that my feelings for her had grown over the past few weeks in her company. I'd spent the last couple of years since my divorce keeping my emotions on lockdown, saving whatever I had for Owen because I'd been wary of another woman taking advantage of me the way Alyssa had.

But Stevie was the antithesis of my ex. Her heart was good and pure. Her intentions equally so, which made opening up my own heart to her, and trusting her, far easier than I'd ever anticipated, despite our short time together as a couple. Yet for her, I knew she viewed our arrangement as nothing more than a fake relationship with an end date, to make sure there was no negative blowback on me for the custody case.

Somewhere along the way, pretending with Stevie had become very real.

There was so much good in her, and the thought of Alyssa doing anything to demean her character in any way set me on edge. "I'm not dropping this until you tell me what Alyssa said or did to you before she walked out of the ladies' room."

She huffed out a little sigh, and I would have smiled at her little show of defiance if the issue wasn't so serious to me. "She just pointed out that I'm not a good fit for you, and she's not wrong," she said, and before I could respond to that comment, she quickly continued. "And there is something I need to tell you. It's about my past. I didn't think it would matter since our relationship wasn't real, that *this*," she said, waving a hand between us, "was just temporary, but Alyssa dug up some information about me and if she uses it to her advantage, it could affect you."

"Okay," I said, unable to imagine what that could be.

She swallowed hard, and though her eyes were steady on mine, I saw the flicker of something vulnerable in her gaze that made my chest tighten. "Do you remember our first night together, on the drive to your place, when you asked me about my parents and I told you they were both gone?"

I nodded. "Yes."

"I lied," she said, and before I could react to that, she quickly went on, as if she wanted to get all of the truth out in the open without any interruptions. "I lied because…my father was an abusive and drunk asshole my entire life and took his anger out on my mother, who was so afraid of him she made excuses for his behavior, but it was bad. We lived in a trailer park, and the circumstances were shitty because we were poor and my father couldn't keep a job because he was an alcoholic. He beat my mother regularly because of his rage issues…until one day he went too far and choked her to death."

I stared at her in shock, because that was the last thing I'd expected to hear.

She took advantage of me processing that information and continued in a rush. "So, yes, while my mother is gone, my father is serving a life sentence in prison for her murder. Valerie and I left Connecticut and moved to New York because we wanted to sever all ties to our father," she said, her voice hoarse and her entire demeanor stiff, which I hated. "I know that this isn't something that could negatively impact your custody case, not when your own twin is in prison for some pretty heinous crimes of his own—"

"I agree," I interrupted her, before she kept rambling. "I'd be lying if I said I wasn't shocked because this was the last thing I'd expected to hear, but you're right. I doubt this is something that would be detrimental to the custody case, so what's the issue, Stevie?" I asked, because she was clearly very upset.

She wrung her hands in her lap. "Alyssa now knows all this and insinuated that 'once the word gets out' about my past, where I come from and what my father did, that it's going to make me look like a desperate gold digger who latched onto you for your money…and she's not wrong about that perception."

I laughed harshly and shook my head at my ex's last-ditch efforts to try and undermine what I had with Stevie. "The only one here that is desperate is Alyssa."

"But it's true how things could look," Stevie insisted, her fingers still twisting together anxiously. "And the thought of my past creating some kind of scandal for you…"

Reaching out, I cupped the side of her face in my palm, then stroked my thumb along her cheek in an attempt to calm her. "Do you honestly believe I give a shit what other people think about me or anything else in my personal life? *I* know who you are, Stevie, and it's never been a gold digger or the kind of woman who would ever take advantage of me, and that's all that matters to me when it comes to *us*." I emphasized that word, wanting her to know we were in this together, whether she realized it yet or not.

"We all have pasts, and yours and mine are not pretty," I went on. "But you have to know that I understand about your father because of my own situation with Lance. I just wish you would have trusted me enough to tell me before now."

"I know," she said, and ducked her head. "It's not something I'm proud of when it comes to my family, and I didn't think my past was relevant to our arrangement."

I lifted her chin back up so her eyes met mine. "That's where you're wrong, Stevie. Everything about you is important and relevant to me," I said, meaning it.

She gave me a small, regret-filled sigh. "I'm sorry…I didn't want such an amazing night like tonight to end like this, with such a serious and uncomfortable discussion."

"Tonight isn't over, and we can end it however we like," I countered, unwilling to let my ex's vindictive behavior ruin anything. In fact, I was more than ready to leave the conversation behind for now and focus on the only thing that mattered to me tonight. Stevie.

Before she could argue, I smiled at her and let my fingers trail lightly down the side of her neck. Her eyes darkened with desire, and I watched as she shivered and her nipples peaked against the soft cotton T-shirt she wore—the exact reaction I was hoping for.

"Given the choice, I want tonight to end with me buried deep inside of you, and you coming around my cock," I murmured huskily. "Preferably with you screaming my name."

She bit her bottom lip and blushed adorably, my dirty talk doing the trick of putting her in a completely different frame of mind. "That would be my choice, too."

Decision made, I stood up and so did she. Taking her hand in mine, I led her back to my bedroom. Once there, I pulled her shirt over her head and tossed it to the floor, leaving her in just her panties. Then, I framed her face in my hands and kissed her, slow and soft and sweet. Her lips parted on a moan, and I swept my tongue inside her mouth, keeping things at a languid, unhurried pace.

After a few minutes of slow, deep kisses, she pressed her palms against my bare chest and gyrated her lower body against mine, making inarticulate noises in the back of her throat. The kind of needy, impatient sounds I was striving for.

I'd imagined under regular circumstances that our night would have ended much differently, with wild, hot, filthy sex. The kind that was fast and hard and primitive because of how greedy and insatiable she made me feel. That's mostly how it had been between us since our first night together—uninhibited, mindless, I-can't-keep-my-hands-off-you, orgasm-inducing fucking.

But tonight, my only goal was to make love to Stevie. To take my time, despite *her* impatience, and savor everything about her. To make her feel special, and adored, and most importantly, chase away any of those insecurities that Alyssa had planted in her head.

I wanted every last one of those vulnerabilities gone, and when I was done with her tonight, I didn't want her to have a single doubt in her mind that she was mine, in every way that mattered. The words would come next, when she was ready to hear them. I had every intention of rectifying this temporary arrangement of ours once the custody case was over in a few weeks. When Stevie would be more apt to believe my intentions toward her were real and true and not all part of some fake relationship ruse I'd paid her for.

But for right now, I was going to show her without words what she meant to me. I was going to shake things up and spend the next hour unraveling every part of her, until she was stripped down to nothing more than raw, intense emotion. So that when I finally slid inside of her, there would be no doubt in her mind who she belonged to.

Me.

I lifted my mouth from hers and looked at her beautifully flushed face. Her eyes were heavy-lidded and glazed over with desire as I slipped my hands into the waistband of her panties and pushed them down her legs until she was completely naked.

"Get up on the bed and spread your legs for me," I ordered gruffly, while I removed my sweatpants.

She did as I ordered, her head resting on the pillows, and her parted thighs giving me a breath-stealing view of her glistening sex. I moved up onto the mattress, and starting at one upraised knee, I trailed hot, damp kisses downward, mixing it up with a few love bites that made her gasp and the scratch of my stubble abrading her skin so she'd feel those chafe marks later. Reaching her pussy, I settled onto my stomach and slowly, leisurely, swiped my tongue through her folds, intending to be down here for a good long while.

She moaned, her fingers sliding through my hair and her hips shamelessly angling upward for more pressure, more friction. In time, when she was finally begging for release, I gave her both, loving the way she cried out my name as her body shuddered from the force of her first orgasm.

Then, I immediately started all over again, licking, sucking, tongue swirling over and around her clit while two fingers fucked her slow and deep to rekindle those intense sensations. It took longer to get her there this second time, but when I did her fingers gripped my hair as she bucked against my mouth, a hoarse cry of bliss escaping her throat.

Her body went lax, then tensed back up when I stayed right where I was, looking up at her from between her spread thighs and making her watch as my tongue did wicked things to her pussy and the tips of my fingers dragged along that sensitive spot inside her body.

She whimpered, her fingers twisting in my hair in an attempt to pull my head away. "Caleb…I can't."

"You can," I rasped, intending to prove her wrong as I pulled her clit between my lips and lashed it with my tongue, making her shudder and moan. "You *will*, because I'm not leaving this spot until you give me *all* your pleasure."

She made a soft, mewling sound and shook her head against the pillows. "I want you inside of me."

"You'll get my cock when I'm good and ready to give it to you," I growled against her pussy, ignoring how said dick ached and throbbed with the need to feel her internal muscles gripping me. "Now, be a good girl, stop fighting me, and give me what *I* want."

I slowed things down, softening my touch until I felt her relax and give herself over to my ministrations. A short while later her hips started gyrating again, seeking firmer pressure against her clit, a deeper penetration of my fingers. I knew her body well, having learned all those little nuances that told me she was heading toward another climax—the soft panting of her breath, the arch of her back, the way her thighs tensed before she clutched the bed covers in her fists and I felt those rippling spasms around my thrusting fingers.

Before the sensations ebbed, I was up and over her, my thick, rigid cock easily gliding into her body and filling her up. I'd never been so grateful that we'd discussed not needing a condom a few weeks ago, because this…*fuck*, being inside of her bare was goddamn sublime.

I groaned and thrust into her, feeling those last little internal contractions milking my cock and knowing I wasn't going to last long. Her fingers pushed through my hair, bringing my mouth down to hers. She kissed me deep and wild, and linked her ankles together just beneath my ass so every time I slammed into her she dragged me in even deeper.

Then it was me who was panting, shuddering, *fucking unraveling* as my orgasm tore through me in sharp, delicious spikes of pleasure. I released everything I had deep inside of her, then collapsed on top of her, doing my best to keep most of my weight on my forearms to keep from crushing her.

Breathing hard, I buried my face against her neck. "You're fucking mine," I growled possessively.

I heard her light, amused laughter as her fingers stroked down my spine. "Okay, caveman."

She thought I was joking, being a Neanderthal after sex, but she'd find out soon enough just how serious I was.

CHAPTER SIXTEEN

Stevie

I STARED AT the document on my computer at the end of the workday on Wednesday, studying all the various taglines the team for PureGlow and I had brainstormed for the client's campaign. Having analyzed all of them a gazillion times, my tired mind drifted, and I wasn't all that surprised which direction it chose to go…replaying that unforgettable Saturday night in Caleb's bed.

My cheeks warmed when I recalled how relentless he'd been, his mouth and fingers doing things to my body no man had ever achieved. Sex with Caleb was always off-the-charts amazing. He was a generous lover, and I'd never been so thoroughly blissed out with orgasms, one after the other, in his incessant pursuit of my pleasure.

The chafe marks he'd left on my thighs kept the reminder fresh in my mind for a few days, but even now, with the tenderness gone, I couldn't stop thinking about that night, beyond the physical gratification. How, after I'd shared my past with him, he'd taken his time like he never had before, worshipping my body, building the intensity and intimacy between us in a way that made me feel as though I'd been free falling through each and every all-consuming climax.

That night with Caleb had felt...different. He'd replaced our normal urgency with something slower, more personal, and caring. As if he'd been striving to establish a deeper trust between us after I'd shared my painful past with him. And, as hard as I'd tried to keep my guard up with Caleb, that vulnerable connection had chipped away at the walls I'd tried so hard to keep in place around him, because falling in love with a man as decent and kind and honorable as him had been incredibly easy to do.

But those deep-seated insecurities were still there, always lurking beneath the surface, refusing to be ignored. How could they not be when my biggest fears still remained, that despite everything, was I really a suitable woman who could mesh seamlessly into Caleb's world beyond our agreement? Probably not, because Alyssa's words that night at the gala, while cruel, held a lot of validity...

"Caleb's money went a long way in making you look like you belong in our world, but let's be honest. Trailer park trash like you will never fit in."

Those words stung, but I couldn't deny the bitter truth in them. Caleb's wealth, his status, his influence...it all went a long way in making someone like me *appear* to belong. When in reality, all it did was mask the fact that I was an outsider with trailer park roots.

I was grateful that Caleb had Owen this week, which limited my alone time with him—and no more sex to convolute things even more. For the remainder of our time together I'd hold up my end of the bargain and keep up appearances, while making sure I kept my heart and emotions out of the equation as much as possible.

A knock on my office door startled me out of my thoughts, and I glanced up and saw Jack standing there.

"Hey, I just wanted to say that you put together a fantastic PowerPoint for PureGlow. They'll be impressed at tomorrow's meeting," he said, then glanced at his watch. "Since everything is ready to go, why don't you get out of here on time for a change?"

"Okay," I said, and shut things down while Jack continued walking down the hallway, his next stop undoubtedly Valerie's desk.

With my computer off and files put away, I grabbed my purse and followed Jack in the same direction. I had to smile when I saw him exactly where I'd suspected, talking to my sister, who smiled up at Jack in a way that told any onlooker that she was completely smitten with him.

"Are you ready to head out?" I asked Valerie, which was our normal routine, to catch the subway together back to the apartment.

"Jack and I were going to go and grab a bite to eat for dinner," she said, looking torn. "Is that okay?"

I rolled my eyes. "Of course it's okay for you to have a life of your own," I said playfully.

I'd be out this evening myself, as well, since I had my own plans to have dinner with Caleb and Owen. I'd already skipped Monday and Tuesday with the excuse of working extra hours to perfect the Power-Point presentation. Caleb had been understanding, even while I'd heard the disappointment in his voice. But for me, I knew it was the right thing to do to establish that emotional distance I desperately needed between us.

I smiled at Valerie. "You two enjoy yourselves."

"We will," Jack said, and grinned at me, a teasing sparkle in his eye. "And don't worry, I'll have her home at a decent hour."

"You'd better," I retorted cheekily.

I left the two of them and took the elevator down to the lobby, then walked out to the street. At five fifteen in the afternoon, the sidewalk was already busy with people heading in the same direction that I was…to the subway.

I'd only taken a few steps when a hand grabbed my arm and hauled me back toward the building. Startled by the unexpected manhandling, I gasped, and when I turned my head, I saw that it was Mark who'd stopped me. Surprise rippled through me, that he'd be so bold as to approach me so aggressively in public.

"Where the fuck is she?" he demanded to know. "I figure since I can't find her and she won't pick up my calls, then I'll just get what I need from you."

Surprisingly, Mark looked well put together in a tailored business suit, but my heart leapt in my chest at the anger blazing in his eyes, and the threat in his voice. It took all my effort to remain calm even while I yanked my arm out of his grasp, which wasn't easy to do considering how strong his grip was. I was probably going to end up with a bruise.

I jutted my chin out angrily. "First of all, don't ever touch me again," I said, well aware that this confrontation could have ended very differently if Valerie had accompanied me out of the building. Even still, she was probably only a few minutes behind me with Jack, and no way did I want Mark to see her and know where she was working so he could stalk her here.

"And second of all, in case you need reminding, a restraining order means stay the hell away from her," I snapped. "She doesn't want anything to do with you or your so-called groveling or apologies."

I tried to step around him, but he moved in the same direction, blocking me from moving away from where he had me backed up against the glass window of the building. A small twinge of fear took hold. The people walking by didn't pay us much attention. It was New York City, after all, and most everyone chose to mind their own business, rather than insert themselves in a hostile situation.

"You're such a bitch," he hissed furiously. "If you don't tell me where she is, I'm going to make life very difficult for you."

I grasped all the bravado I could muster. "Fuck

you, Mark. Leave her alone and get a life. Your stalking behavior is pathetic, and so are you."

This time, I pushed my way past him, but I only made it two steps before I felt his hands on my back. Before I could do anything, he shoved me hard, propelling me forward faster than my heels could keep up, and I went flying. I tried to catch myself, but ended up landing on my hands and knees on the sidewalk, the impact jarring my entire body. The scrape of the concrete against my palms and exposed knees from my skirt had me crying out, along with the pain I felt radiating up my left arm from my wrist.

"What the fuck, man?" a deep, intimidating voice called out, clearly talking to Mark.

Random people walked past me without helping, and I glanced up to see a burly man heading toward me after witnessing what had just happened. His gaze narrowed on Mark as that chicken shit darted toward the curb, hailed a cab, and quickly got inside before my rescuer could stop him. Good thing, because the guy was solid muscle and was built like an MMA fighter.

The guy crouched in front of me, genuine concern on his face. "Are you okay?"

Tears sprang to my eyes. Not because I thought I was seriously injured, but the embarrassment of the situation was starting to sink in. I swallowed back the lump in my throat, trying to speak, but unable to.

"Jesus," the man said upon seeing my distress. Very gently, he grabbed my arm to assist me back to my feet, holding me steady until my heels stopped wobbling. "What can I do to help? Do you need an EMT?"

I shook my head. I was scraped up for sure, and my wrist hurt like hell, but nothing was seriously broken that I could tell. "You've already helped by stepping in," I said gratefully. "I work in this building, so I'm going to go back inside and up to my office."

The man frowned. "Are you sure you're okay on your own?"

I managed a small smile, appreciating his concern. "I am. Thank you for your help."

The guy made sure I was safely in the lobby before he continued on his way, and just as I reached the elevators, one of them opened and Jack and Valerie stepped off the lift, my sister laughing at something Jack had just said. As soon as she saw me, cradling my left hand and my palms and knees bloodied, all her amusement died.

"What happened?" she asked, her eyes wide with worry. "Did you trip and fall?"

I hated to have to tell her the truth. "Not on my own. Mark was waiting outside when I walked out of the building and he cornered me, then demanded to know where to find you," I said, watching as panic immediately transformed Valerie's expression. "I managed to push past him, but he shoved me from behind and I, well, as you can see, I didn't fall gracefully," I said, attempting to inject some humor into the situation to calm my sister down, which didn't help.

"What the *fuck*," Jack said, his eyes blazing with

fury. "Tell me where I can find this prick so I can knock some sense into him."

I shook my head. "You're not getting involved, Jack," I said, even though I honestly didn't know how it was going to end with Mark, who had no issues violating his restraining order. But I also knew I needed to report this assault, to show how his harassment was escalating.

My sister grabbed my hands to check my scraped palms, and I sucked in a sharp breath as I felt another jolt of pain in my wrist. At Valerie's worried look, I quickly tried to reassure her. "I'm fine."

"Clearly, you're not." Jack frowned at me. "There's an urgent care right up the street. Let's go," he said, taking charge.

I knew it was the smart thing to do considering the throb in my wrist was increasing, so I didn't argue further. "I was supposed to have dinner with Caleb and Owen tonight. I need to let him know I'm not going to make it."

"I'll text him and tell him you had an accident and we're taking you to urgent care," Valerie said, rummaging in my purse and retrieving my cellphone to do just that.

I settled into the back of the cab Jack managed to hail for us, too exhausted to argue.

CHAPTER SEVENTEEN

Caleb

I'D JUST GOTTEN home and relieved Tillie from watching Owen for the afternoon when I received a text message on my phone.

This is Valerie. Stevie had an accident and Jack and I are taking her to urgent care to make sure she's okay. She wanted to let you know that she won't be able to make it for dinner tonight.

What the hell? What kind of accident? My heart seemed to slam against my chest, and I immediately called Stevie's phone because I didn't have the patience to get information through texts, and it was Valerie who picked up.

"What do you mean she had an accident, and why does she need to go to urgent care?" I demanded to know more harshly than I'd intended. I wasn't a man prone to panic, but then again, the word "accident" was too damn vague for me and worst-case scenarios were filling up my mind faster than I could sort through them.

"She had an altercation with my ex just outside of

work," Valerie said, sounding upset. "She's mostly okay. Scraped hands and knees and she says her wrist hurts, so we just want to make sure it's not broken."

"I'm coming down to urgent care," I said, my only thought to see for myself that Stevie's injuries were minor. "Which one is it?"

I heard Valerie relay that message to Stevie, then she came back on the phone with her sister's reply.

"Stevie asked that you please don't come down here. She's insisting that it's not that serious, and there's nothing you can do for her here, anyway. We're walking in now, so I need to go and get Stevie checked in. She said she'll let you know when we're back home."

The line disconnected before I could demand more answers, and for the next two and a half hours it was all I could do to remain calm—making dinner for Owen and getting him through his evening routine— and not ignore Stevie's request to stay home.

Frustration coursed through me. It had already been a helluva week, and it was only Wednesday. On Monday, I'd talked to Remy about the prescription pills Stevie had seen Alyssa taking at the gala, and just as I thought, as much as Remy wanted to help, there was nothing he could do to find out what medications my ex was currently taking to rule out the possibility of anything addicting.

So, yesterday, I'd made the difficult, and only, decision to call Alyssa's parents to discuss the possible issue with them, which hadn't gone over well. It had been an awkward and tense conversation, with her mother, Joyce, accusing me of trying to malign their daughter's character, which I found laughable considering what Alyssa had done to Stevie the night of the gala.

I'd expressed my concerns based on Alyssa's behavior, and even the few times that Owen had told me about Alyssa not feeling well and him staying with his grandparents during the weeks that she had him because she was sleeping so much. Reluctantly, Joyce finally admitted that Alyssa was dealing with anxiety and depression, which meant maybe, possibly, *hopefully* those pills she'd been taking were nothing more than a prescription to help with those issues.

I wasn't fully convinced, but it was all I had to go on. I'd expected a phone call from a pissed-off Alyssa, telling me to stay out of her business, but, surprisingly, I hadn't heard from her. Which made me wonder if her parents had kept our phone conversation, and my worries, to themselves. And if so, maybe they were more concerned about their daughter than they'd let on.

As the time dragged on while I waited for Stevie to return home from urgent care, I constantly checked my phone for messages, anxious for an update on her condition and my stomach in knots. I allowed Owen to play twenty minutes of Minecraft before it was time for bed, while I paced restlessly in front of the floor-to-ceiling windows in my living room. I dragged my fingers through my hair for the umpteenth time, feeling helpless and beyond furious that this ex of Valerie's had dared to touch Stevie in any way.

From what I understood, the restraining order against Mark was for Valerie, so he hadn't violated any laws in that regard by approaching Stevie, though an altercation was possible grounds for an assault charge, and an arrest if he was responsible for Stevie's injuries. I needed to know the details, because whoever this asshole was, I was going to make sure he understood that I was far more intimidating and powerful than a fucking restraining order. That if he came near Valerie or Stevie again, there would be hell to pay.

At ten after eight, I finally received a text from Stevie's phone, brief and to the point. *I'm home and I'm fine. I'm exhausted and I'll talk to you tomorrow.*

My jaw clenched, hating how guarded and emotionally withdrawn she'd been with me since Saturday night, and there was no way I wasn't going to see for myself that she was *fine*, as she'd put things. I was so wound up, and I refused to wait another minute to find out what the hell happened.

I called Cara to stay with Owen, and after she arrived I strode down to Stevie and Valerie's apartment, knocking briskly on the door.

Jack, the guy Valerie was dating, appeared on the other side, and I was grateful that he'd stayed with the two of them at urgent care and made sure they'd gotten home safely.

The other man gave me a smirk. "Stevie did warn us after sending you that last text message to expect you, despite her saying she'd talk to you tomorrow." His tone was filled with humor.

I was far from amused as I walked into the apartment behind Jack, seeing only Valerie sitting on the living room couch. "Where is she?" I asked, feeling anxious that Stevie was nowhere in sight to reassure me that she truly was okay.

"She's taking a shower," Valerie replied. "She's scraped up from the fall, and she did sprain her left wrist, but nothing is broken."

Relief flooded through me, along with sheer determination to put an end to this guy's harassment, by any means necessary. I sat down in a chair across from where Jack and Valerie were seated on the sofa. "Tell me everything that happened."

Valerie was more forthcoming with the details, while I knew that Stevie would have downplayed the situation. By the time Valerie finished relaying the story of her ex confronting Stevie before shoving her to the ground because she wouldn't give him the information he wanted on Valerie, my entire body vibrated with anger.

"What's Mark's last name?" I asked Valerie, prepared to have Remy find out whatever he could on this guy to use to my advantage before I paid him a personal visit myself.

"Branson," Valerie said.

That brought me up short, and I stared at her in disbelief. "Branson…as in The Branson Group?"

She nodded. "Yes. I used to work there. That's

how I met Mark."

Holy shit, I thought, putting the pieces together in my mind. Mark Branson...the son of Grant Branson, the CEO of The Branson Group, a financial investment firm I was well acquainted with. The leverage I needed had just fallen into my lap in the most karmic way.

Out of the corner of my eye, I saw Stevie walk into the main living area, wearing an old T-shirt and a pair of pink, well-worn sweatpants. Her hair was damp, and her left wrist was encased in a black brace. When she saw me, she sighed in resignation.

I immediately jumped up from the couch and approached her, my eyes checking her out from head to toe, just in case the doctor missed anything. I didn't bother to ask if she was okay, because I knew I'd get a very pat, "I'm fine", response.

"Are you in pain?" I asked instead, also seeing the red scratches on her palms. It took everything in me not to pick up her hands and hold them in mine, or just touch her in general. But I heeded her body language, which was extremely guarded.

She shrugged. "My left wrist is a little uncomfortable. I took a few ibuprofens so I can sleep."

I frowned at her weary expression, at the fatigue I could see in her eyes. There was no telling how many aches and pains she'd be feeling by morning. "Maybe you should stay home from work tomorrow."

Her chin lifted a fraction, and she gave me one of those "you're not the boss of me" looks that would have made me laugh under different circumstances. "I have a presentation tomorrow and I'm not calling in sick."

"The team can handle the presentation," Jack offered. "Samantha and Brandy would certainly understand."

"No, I'll be there," Stevie insisted, stubborn as ever.

"Okay, but if you wake up in the morning and don't feel up to it and change your mind—"

"I won't," she reiterated, then shifted her gaze back to me, a slight smile on her lips as if to soften her next words. "I'm really tired and I'm going to bed. Thank you for coming by and checking on me."

I gave her a nod, when all I wanted was to take her home with me, tuck her into my bed where she belonged, and watch over her. But that clearly wasn't an option. "I'm taking care of the Mark situation first thing in the morning."

Her eyes went wide with surprise. "How?"

"I know his father personally." That's all the information Stevie needed, because I knew she wouldn't approve of what I had in mind.

A small frown formed between her brows and I knew she was considering telling me to stay out of it. *Not a chance*, I thought, but I waited for her reply. Finally, she sighed in what seemed like acceptance.

"Well, I hope whatever you say to him works better than a restraining order."

Thank goodness common sense had won out. I

didn't want to argue with her tonight. "Oh, it will," I promised.

Uncaring that the two other people in the room were watching, I finally gave in to the urge to reach out and lightly caress my fingers along Stevie's cheek. She instinctively softened at my touch, and *almost* leaned into my hand before she caught herself and slowly pulled back.

So, I did the same. For now. "Get some rest and I'll check in with you tomorrow."

THE NEXT MORNING, I strode into The Branson Group and up to the receptionist's desk. Brittany, who I was well acquainted with since she'd been there for a few years, greeted me with a smile.

"Hi, Mr. Kane," she said, then tipped her head in confusion as her eyes seemed to go over a document on her computer screen. "I don't have you on the schedule for a meeting this morning. Is Mr. Branson expecting you?"

"No," I said amicably. "This is a visit on a personal matter. Can you let him know it's urgent that I speak to him?"

Yes, it was presumptuous of me to show up and demand to see the CEO of the firm, but when a company retained tens of millions of my dollars, I had every right to be confident of my ability to command an impromptu meeting with Grant Branson.

Sure enough, after a brief conversation on the phone, Brittany flashed me another smile. "He'll see you in his office," she said, not bothering to get up from her seat to escort me since I'd been there dozens of times before.

"Thank you." I headed toward the suite of executive offices, to the one with a panoramic view of New York City.

I walked inside Grant's office and closed the door behind me since nobody else needed to be privy to this conversation, before approaching his desk. Grant stood up and reached across his desk to shake my hand. He was an older man, probably close to the same age my father would have been, with distinguished graying hair and pale blue eyes that were filled with curiosity, and maybe a bit of concern, for my unscheduled visit.

"Caleb, it's always great to see you, but this is unexpected," he said, as he sat down in the leather chair behind his desk, and I settled into one across from him. "Is there an issue with your portfolio?"

"Not at the moment," I said in a neutral tone. "But that will depend on how this meeting goes."

Grant frowned, the concern in his eyes unmistakable. "I didn't realize you were unhappy with our advice and management of your investments."

"I wasn't, until some recent events were brought to my attention, which have to do with your son, Mark."

"Mark?" Grant repeated, looking thoroughly confused. "He's only a junior advisor and doesn't handle your investments."

"Oh, I know that," I said, then asked, "Are you familiar with the name Valerie Palmer?"

He grimaced. "Yes. Mark dated her for a while. I know they had a rocky breakup, which then started affecting her work here at the firm and we had to let her go. All the more reason to adopt a no-office-romance policy."

The last bit was said with a bit of humor, and I didn't care for the fact that the blame was laid on Valerie. "Is that what Mark told you? That she wasn't able to do her job because of their breakup?"

Grant must have heard the thread of anger in my tone, because he sat up straighter, his demeanor tensing. "What does any of this have to do with your investments?"

"Good question, and I'll get to that in a minute." I gave him a tight smile. "Here's what I know and believe, based on your son's recent actions. He dated Valerie, but he was also abusive to her in that relation-ship—"

"Wait a minute," Grant said, interrupting me. "That's quite an accusation you're making against my son."

I didn't back off, considering the proof against Mark…and then it occurred to me that Grant might not even know about his son's less-than-sterling behavior. "Are you aware that Mark has a restraining order against him, filed by Valerie?"

Grant went quiet, but the *oh shit* look on his face

spoke volumes.

"If you didn't know—because why would a grown man tell his father something embarrassing like that?—I can assure you that he does have a restraining order against him. And he's violated it by stalking Valerie and contacting her by phone."

"How do you know this?" Grant asked, his shock still apparent.

"Because Valerie's sister, Stevie, is my girlfriend," I told him. "And yesterday, your son assaulted Stevie outside her workplace after demanding to know where to find Valerie. She ended up with scrapes and bruises and a sprained wrist."

Grant scrubbed a hand along his face and shook his head, looking appalled. "I…I had no idea."

Sadly, I believed him, and I was glad that he didn't try and make excuses for Mark's behavior. However, that didn't change the ultimatum I was about to issue. "Regardless, as much as I appreciate our working relationship and the firm's management of my investments, if you don't handle your son's inability to stay away from Valerie and Stevie, I will have no issues pulling my portfolio and taking it elsewhere. And if I do that, you can be assured that my partner, Beck Daniels, will do the same, along with any other person I've recommended to this firm…which I'll no longer be able to do when it employs such an unstable financial advisor."

Much to Grant's credit, he took my ultimatum seriously, probably because he realized how much he,

CARLY PHILLIPS & ERIKA WILDE

and his firm, had to lose. "I'm very sorry about this," he said, his apology genuine. "I know Mark has had anger issues stemming from my nasty divorce with his mother a few years ago, but I had no idea he'd abused Valerie." The man visibly shuddered. "Or that he has a restraining order against him. You can rest assured I'll take care of the issue immediately."

Satisfied with his response, I stood up. "I hope you do. If Mark so much as tries to contact Valerie again, in any way, shape, or form, or approaches my girl-friend, Stevie, we're done."

Grant stood up, too, and nodded. "I understand."

I reached across the desk and shook his hand again out of respect for our current relationship, then left his office, certain Grant would do everything in his power to make sure that his son didn't fuck up one of the firm's biggest accounts, and Mark left innocent women alone.

CHAPTER EIGHTEEN

Stevie

AFTER AN EXHAUSTING week, between work and the incident with Mark—though Caleb hadn't disclosed how he'd taken care of the issue and I really wasn't sure I wanted to know the details—I was actually grateful for the weekend getaway at the Dune Deck Beach Club in the Hamptons that Caleb had planned for Owen's birthday.

Caleb, Owen, Cara, and I had arrived Friday evening, with Remy and Raven driving separately and meeting us for dinner at a nearby restaurant before we all headed to the club to check in for the weekend. I shared a two-bedroom suite with Cara that had a breathtaking ocean view, while Caleb and Owen stayed in a similar room next to ours.

The exclusivity of the club wasn't lost on me, and when we arrived that initial imposter syndrome was strong. It was difficult not to be aware of all the luxurious amenities, along with the caliber of upper-class and wealthy members who belonged to the club.

But just like at the gala, the fact that I was with

Caleb Kane—a guest that the employees knew by name—there was an automatic acceptance. No one looked at me twice, or in any way that made me feel as though I didn't belong, which made it much easier to relax and enjoy myself.

Saturday morning we all had breakfast together, then Caleb and Remy took Owen to a nearby family park for a few hours for a round of mini-golf and go-karting, while Raven insisted us girls enjoy a bit of pampering at the spa since my sprained wrist wasn't conducive to handle those more challenging and fun games. We opted for pedicures, then met up with the boys for a bite to eat once they returned.

After lunch, Raven, Cara, and I took Owen down to the beach while the men went to the lounge to watch a football game. While Cara and Owen kicked around a beach ball on the sand, Raven and I reclined on lounge chairs beneath umbrellas, sipping on fruity drinks that had been delivered to us.

"So, what's going on with you?" Raven asked, setting her drink on the small table between us. "And don't tell me you're fine, because that would be a lie."

It was the first time we'd been alone together since arriving at the Hamptons, and leave it to my best friend to be blunt. "There's just a lot that's happened this past week, as you well know." I lifted my braced hand to make my point.

She didn't look convinced. "Did something happen between you and Caleb? The two of you seem…off, and you especially seem quieter than usual and more closed off."

I glanced out at the ocean and sighed, because I couldn't deny her claim. At least her impression about my mood lately, because I knew I was the one who'd created that divide between myself and Caleb.

Caleb had been nothing but attentive since our night together after the gala, but not in an overbearing way. I knew he was concerned about my wrist, which was still in a brace, but I realized now that the issue with Mark was resolved, Caleb's actions toward me were more…subdued. It was as though he'd taken his cues from me, clearly sensing, and respecting, those walls I'd re-erected to keep my emotions safe from potential heartbreak. Like a man who was completely in tune to my needs, he was giving me space, free from pressure or expectations.

It's what I thought I wanted, that pulling back was necessary…yet I missed our easy flirtations. The way he'd touch me just because he could. How he'd looked at me as if I was the only woman who mattered to him. I still saw glimpses of those things, but it was clear that Caleb was letting me figure things out, without making me feel smothered, which was one of the things I loved about him.

Yes, I loved him, and it made me wonder, despite my misgivings about fitting into his world, if losing Caleb and that deep, undeniable connection between us was worth it. Was I letting my pride and insecurities get in the way of what could be the greatest love of my life? But then again, I really had no idea where I stood with Caleb, and what would happen once the custody case was over.

"Hey, are you still with me?" Raven snapped her fingers in front of me.

I blinked, realizing that I'd zoned out and she was still waiting for an answer. "Sorry," I said, shaking my head.

"Yeah, not sure where you disappeared to, but welcome back," she joked.

I exhaled a deep breath before speaking and giving Raven the truth. "You asked if something happened between Caleb and I, and honestly, the issue is me," I admitted.

"You?" Her brows rose. "How so?"

"After my run-in with Alyssa at the gala, I can't deny she planted doubts and insecurities about not being the kind of woman who blended into Caleb's world, because of how I grew up, and feeling like an outsider looking in." I stared at my newly painted pink toenails for a few beats, before shifting my gaze back to Raven's. "I mean, those doubts were always there, but I'd be lying if I said she didn't amplify them."

Raven tipped her head. "And what kind of woman are you referring to, who would be a better match for Caleb?"

I shrugged. "Someone sophisticated and worldly, who knows all the etiquette and formalities of being with an obscenely wealthy man like Caleb."

Raven rolled her eyes, that sarcasm transferring to her voice when she said, "Yeah, because Caleb marrying someone from his social circle worked out really well the first time."

"You know what I mean," I said, shifting restlessly on the lounge chair.

"Let me tell you what I do know," Raven said, her expression completely serious. "As you're already aware, I've lived two separate lives, one with money, and one without, so I know what it's like to have those insecurities. I was adopted into the Kane family, but I was never embraced by a mother who should have loved me regardless of who I am. I was raised with all the luxuries money could buy, but was never accepted in the way I craved but rather made to feel like I was a burden, not to mention responsible for Lance's behavior when he assaulted me the first time, when I was a teenager."

I held back a reaction because I knew the story and understood it was a sensitive one for Raven.

"What I do know," she went on, "and learned from Cassandra and Lance, is that money and wealth doesn't give you integrity. It doesn't give you morals or decency. You could be dirt poor or filthy rich, but if you don't have those core values, then what kind of person are you? You're someone like Cassandra, or Alyssa, who is self-centered and a bitch who has to put others down to feel better about themselves."

Raven's gaze suddenly softened as she continued. "Then you have men like Caleb, and Remy, who are honorable, ethical, and dependable. Men who don't judge a person for things that are out of their control, like my past with Lance, and yours with your father. They don't give a shit about those things when it comes to the women they care about."

I swallowed hard, Raven's words resonating deep inside of me.

"There are always going to be insecure women like Alyssa who will try to bring other women down," she went on. "All that should matter to you is what Caleb thinks, and I already know by the way he looks at you and treats you, he's crazy about you. Now, it's up to you to believe that you're enough for him just as you are, that you deserve a man who makes you happy, no matter his social standing, without any doubts or insecurities getting in the way of your happiness."

My heart pounded in my chest as I realized that was exactly what I was doing. Allowing my feelings of inadequacy to keep me from taking that final leap of faith with Caleb. To trust that a man like him, who'd already proven himself in so many ways, would love me just as I was.

Even though I had no alone time with Caleb, Raven's advice stayed with me for the rest of the afternoon and evening, and through to the next morning when everyone met down in the restaurant for brunch to celebrate Owen's seventh birthday. As our small group was led to a more private area of the dining room, Caleb smiled at me and placed a hand low on my back as we walked in that direction—not because it was expected, but because I knew it was something that was just instinctual for him, and because he wanted to touch me, to let me know he cared despite the fact that I'd pulled back due to my insecurities and fears.

Feeling as though I'd made some kind of mental and emotional breakthrough after my conversation with Raven the previous day, I was anxious to talk to Caleb, to tell him that I didn't want *us* to be over after the custody case. Here in the Hamptons, with Owen and family around, it wasn't the place to have that discussion, but I was prepared to fight for all the things Caleb had silently offered me—protection, a safe space, and the kind of emotional security I'd never had before. He'd given me all those things, and so much more, and I'd be a fool to let my pride get in the way of something so special and rare. And I needed to tell him that I wanted us, that I wanted *him*, and everything that came with being a part of his life.

He glanced at me as we sat next to each other, and I smiled at him—not the kind of obligatory smile I'd been resorting to all week because of those walls I'd erected, but a real and intimate one that softened my features and hopefully conveyed my willingness to let him in.

He tipped his head, as if sensing the change in me. "I take it you slept well last night?" he asked as everyone else settled into their seats, with Owen sitting beside me at the end of the table.

"I would have slept better in your bed, with you," I teased in a whisper, giving him enough to realize that I was also completely serious.

His gaze searched mine, and I saw the hopeful look in his eyes as he reached down and took my good hand, weaving our fingers intimately together. The gesture conveyed affection and tenderness, comfort and reassurance, and I opened myself to all those things with him.

"You and I need to talk," he said.

We hadn't really "talked" much over the past week because I hadn't allowed it, but he obviously saw an opening he didn't want to let slip though his fingers. Usually *we need to talk* came with an adverse implication, but I had a feeling that Caleb and I were finally, hopefully, on the same page.

"Yes, we do," I agreed.

For the next hour, it was all about celebrating Owen's birthday. The adults ordered brunch entrees, and pancakes for Owen, followed by a chocolate cake with candles. The presents everyone had brought for the occasion were unwrapped, revealing Lego sets, superhero figurines, Minecraft gear, and a Nerf gun from his uncle Remy.

"They're right over there," a familiar female voice said in a loud, demanding tone, interrupting our festivities. "I can see them in that room and I want to wish my son a happy birthday."

My stomach pitched, already knowing who it was before we all glanced in Alyssa's direction, watching her approach—a bit unsteadily—with a hostess trying to dissuade her. The same man I'd seen at the gala with her trailed a few feet behind, clearly looking uncomfortable with the scene she was making.

"I'm very sorry, Mr. Kane," the hostess said as they reached us. "I'll go get the manager."

"It's *fine*," Alyssa insisted irritably, shooing away the young girl with her hand. Then she dropped her purse on the end of the table and held her arms out toward Owen. "Come here and give your mother a hug."

Owen shook his head and shrank away from Alyssa and toward me, pressing against me, like he'd seen this side of his mother before and it scared him. I wrapped an arm protectively around him, refusing to let Alyssa near him, and the look she gave me was pure disdain.

Caleb abruptly stood up to diffuse the situation, and even across the table Remy was tense as he watched the scene unfold. The only man who didn't seem poised and ready to interfere was her date. Instead, he stood off to the side, looking embarrassed. Clearly, he didn't have the backbone to deal with Alyssa's bullshit, which was why she was probably with a man like him.

"You need to leave, Alyssa," Caleb said, more calmly than I knew he felt, because he was trying to keep things civil in front of his son.

Cara, as if sensing things were about to escalate, jumped up from her seat and came around to Owen, gently taking his hand. "Hey, Owey, let's take your Nerf gun and go play with it on the beach."

"Okay," he said quietly.

I released him, and he slid off his seat and went with Cara, giving his mother a wide berth as the two of them left the restaurant, and I could understand why. Alyssa's face was flushed, her pupils little pinpoints, and she overall seemed agitated and unstable.

"Are you serious?" She whirled on Caleb furiously. "I can't even wish my son a happy birthday?"

Caleb came around to the front of the table. "You weren't invited, and this is *my* weekend with Owen."

Again, calm and controlled, but I could see the rigid set of his body.

Alyssa rolled her eyes insolently. "In case you've forgotten, I'm still a member at this club, too, so I'm welcome here whenever I want." Her gaze slid past Caleb, to me, a sneer on her lips. "And, really, I belong here more than she does. All this tramp is doing is taking advantage of what your money can buy her. But like I already told her, money can't change where you come from—"

"That's enough," Caleb snapped, and grabbed her arm. While she sputtered protests, he led her through the dining room and out a set of glass doors that led to the patio outside.

The guests in the dining room watched the scene, and the man she'd brought with her grimaced, shifting awkwardly on his feet, but he didn't go to Alyssa's rescue as she yelled at Caleb, which we could all see happening through the glass doors.

"I'm so sorry," the guy finally spoke, his meek demeanor shocking me. "Alyssa was adamant that she'd been invited for brunch for her son's birthday, but clearly, that's not the case, and I apologize."

Raven's lips pursed. "She didn't tell you that Caleb was going to be here?"

He shook his head. "No, just that we were invited for brunch."

"Yeah, well, you might want to go and see if you can calm her down," Remy suggested.

The man frowned as he glanced back at Caleb and Alyssa, and now what looked to be the manager of the club, trying to talk to a hysterical Alyssa. Very reluctantly, he headed in their direction.

As soon as he was gone, Remy grabbed Alyssa's purse, set it on his lap, and started rummaging through the contents.

"What are you doing?" Raven asked, looking and sounding a little shocked at her husband's behavior.

"This," he said, and pulled out a sealed baggie that was filled with prescription bottles and other smaller baggies with various colored pills. "Trying to find the proof that Caleb needs to show that Alyssa is abusing drugs again." He smiled grimly at his wife. "I'm a private investigator and sometimes I have to be a little creative to get the results I need."

Raven and I both gaped at the vast amount of drugs Alyssa had on her.

"Oh, shit," Raven said, echoing my own thoughts.

"Yeah, you could say that." Remy swiped open his cellphone and started taking pictures of everything, including the names and prescriptions on the bottles.

"Jesus," he muttered to himself. "There's oxy, Xanax, tramadol…all prescribed by different doctors. And who the hell knows what's in the smaller, unmarked bags or where she got the pills from."

He finished collecting the evidence, then shoved the large plastic bag back into her oversized designer purse. He set her bag on the table just as our server came by our table.

The young girl grimaced in apology. "I'm so sorry about the disturbance. "I'm just grabbing her purse since our manager is escorting her off the premises."

We all watched through the windows as the server gave Alyssa her bag, while the manager of the club tried to reason with Alyssa, who was livid and still yelling. Surprisingly, it was the guy she'd arrived with who calmed her down with something he said to her, and they finally left.

Caleb came back inside, his expression grim, and I knew it was about to get much worse for him when he learned what Remy had discovered.

CHAPTER NINETEEN

Caleb

I DROVE BACK to my apartment late that Sunday afternoon, exhausted by the events of the past few hours, starting with Alyssa showing up at the club, demanding to see Owen. The fact that Owen had been afraid of his own mother's erratic behavior had been shocking, and revealing, telling me that Owen had most likely experienced this unstable side to Alyssa before.

After the scene Alyssa had made at our table, my only concern was to get her as far away from Owen as possible, and it was when we were outside on the restaurant's patio, with her yelling at me, that I realized she was high on *something*. It wasn't just her frenetic, hysterical, and initially loud protests, but when the guy who'd accompanied her finally came out to talk to her, to try and calm her down when I couldn't, her entire demeanor changed. She'd gone from irritable, to confused, to telling him she felt nauseous. That anxiety Alyssa's mother had mentioned seemed to take hold, and she'd mumbled frantically beneath her breath,

"Where is my purse? I need my purse."

The hostess arrived with her bag, and Alyssa was near tears as she told the manager, who was ready to escort her off the premises, that she needed to use the restroom before they left the club.

The whole scene was bizarre, and concerning.

When I returned to the table, Remy informed me of what he'd found in Alyssa's purse, and the amount of prescription drugs she'd had on her had been alarming. Not to mention all the different pills that were prescribed by various doctors and pain management clinics to feed her addiction. He'd texted me all the photographs he'd taken so I'd have the evidence I needed to take to her parents.

Unfortunately, I had to cut the day at the beach short, asking Remy to take Stevie, Cara, and Owen back home because my only concern was to confront Alyssa's parents with the truth of what had been discovered.

With that done, I'd texted Stevie to let her know that I was heading back to The Cortland, and she asked me to stop by her apartment first, which I would have done anyway since I wanted to tell her what had happened with Alyssa's parents. Not to mention Stevie and I had unresolved issues of our own to discuss.

Cara had Owen at her place, so I had at least the next few hours alone with Stevie. When I reached her apartment and she opened the door, her face lined with worry, all the tension and stress I'd been carrying with me since Alyssa's appearance at the club finally evaporated.

As soon as I stepped inside and the door closed behind us, Stevie slipped her arms around me and held me tight. I didn't hesitate to return the hug, grateful to have her support. The emotional and physical distance she'd put between us was now gone. I didn't know what had happened to change things, but I was beyond relieved to have the Stevie I knew and loved back in my embrace.

"I'm so sorry," she whispered, pulling back just enough to look up at me. "Confronting Alyssa's parents with the truth of their daughter's addiction couldn't have been easy."

"It wasn't," I agreed, "but it had to be done."

She nodded in understanding and took my hand, leading me into the living room. "Valerie is out for the evening with Jack," she said, letting me know it was just the two of us as we sat down side by side on the sofa, her hand still holding mine. "Tell me what happened."

I exhaled a deep breath, and while she quietly listened, I told her the details, starting with Alyssa's parents' initial denial that their daughter had relapsed. But there had been no refuting the proof I had and I'd informed them if they didn't finally do something about Alyssa's addiction and get her back into rehab so she could get the help she needed, then it would be the family court judge who would be viewing the photos next.

That was the last thing her parents wanted, and I'd

CARLY PHILLIPS & ERIKA WILDE

given them three days to get Alyssa checked into rehab. They'd also assured me that they would get Alyssa to drop the custody case, again because they didn't want those photographs exposed. I was fine with that, but assured them that it would be a good long while before Alyssa had joint custody of Owen again. Maybe, in time, supervised visits would be approved, but that wasn't a discussion I'd even consider until I knew with absolute certainty that Alyssa was clean again.

"Are you okay?" Stevie asked once I was done with my story.

I nodded. "Yes. I feel better knowing that I have her parents' cooperation, which is important because I think they are the only ones who will really be able to convince Alyssa she needs to go back to rehab for a longer treatment. They were shocked to see all the prescription drugs she had on her, and they understand my concern is for Owen, and theirs is, as well."

"Good." Stevie squeezed my hand and gave me a soft smile. "I'm glad they were receptive."

I was equally relieved, but now that I'd taken care of that issue and knew I had Alyssa's parents' support, my sole focus was Stevie and getting us back on track. "So, can we talk about what happened between you and me at brunch this morning, before Alyssa arrived?"

She bit her bottom lip a bit nervously and nodded. "Yes. I meant what I said when I agreed that we needed to talk."

"Then tell me what you have to say, because this past week has been pure hell for me without you around," I told her, meaning it. "I don't know what happened for me to get *you* back today, but I'm thankful that you're here and no longer shutting me out. Tell me what changed," I prompted.

She paused, collecting her thoughts. "A conversation with Raven put things into perspective for me and quieted those fears and insecurities of mine," she said softly, quietly. "I can't say that they've disappeared completely, but what I do know is that I'm not willing to let those issues define me when it comes to you, and us, together."

I cocked my head curiously, wanting and needing to know more. "How do you mean?"

She swallowed hard. "You've never made me feel less than beautiful, and perfect. You've never judged me, and you've always made me feel like I belong in every part of your life, despite our differences."

"That's because I don't see differences. I see you for who you are, Stevie," I said truthfully, and reached out to skim my fingers along her jaw. "Not where you've come from or what has happened in your past. I don't give a damn about any of that. All that matters to me is right here." I tapped the left side of her chest, where her heart resided, making my point.

"I know," she said, her voice tight with emotion. "You've proven that to me, in so many ways, but I couldn't see those actions for what they were, or believe that I could truly fit into your life, until Raven made me realize that my insecurities were going to end up costing me the best man I'd ever met."

I couldn't deny the hope that rose inside of me as I searched her gaze. "I want to be everything you need, Stevie. I want to give you anything and everything your heart desires."

She smiled at me, so sweetly. "There is only one thing my heart desires."

"Which is?" I was desperate to hear her say the words.

"Just...*you*," she whispered.

"Stevie...you've had me since our first night together," I told her, needing her to know how quickly and easily I'd fallen for her. "That's all it took for me to realize that I wanted you in my life, but things happened with Alyssa and while we've been going through the motions of what you believe is a fake relationship, it's been anything but that for me."

Her eyes widened in surprise to hear just how long I'd been harboring my feelings for her. "So, now that being together for the custody case is no longer an issue...where do we go from here?" she asked.

I arched an incredulous brow at her. "After all that, you have to ask?"

She shrugged, but I still saw the smallest of vulnerabilities in her gaze. "I need to hear it from you."

"I have something to show you instead." Something that would give her all the proof she needed to know I was in this relationship for the long haul. That my feelings for her were genuinely real.

I surprised her by standing up, and offered my hand to bring her to her feet, too. She stared at me curiously as she followed me up to my apartment. She hadn't been there since before the incident with Mark, and I'd made a distinct change that I knew would shock her, but I also hoped it would show her what she truly meant to me.

I led her into my living room, and because it was dark in the apartment the lamps on the end tables automatically switched on, illuminating the new piece of artwork I'd hung on the wall. When Stevie saw it, she gasped in shock.

"Oh my God," she said, then laughed, a delighted sound I wanted to hear as often as possible. "I can't believe you bought and hung up Fallon's pop art painting in your perfectly neutral-colored penthouse."

I came up behind Stevie, wrapping my arms around her from behind, and she automatically relaxed and leaned back against me. "You're right about something," I admitted, and feigned a sigh. "I could use more fun and color in my life. And this painting, which reminds me of you, will remind me of *that*. Owen loves it, by the way."

She turned her head and glanced up at me. "I hope you enjoy it."

I grinned down at her. "I hope you do, too."

She looked surprised at that and arched a playful brow. "Are you giving me visiting rights?" she teased.

"No, I'm giving it *to* you," I said. "With one condition."

Confusion passed across her features. "Which is?"

I finally released Stevie so I could turn her around to face me. So she could look into my eyes and see how serious I was about her. About us. About a future together.

"My condition is that the painting stays here, right where it is. And you stay here, with me, right where you belong. Because when you look at the painting, and it makes you smile, I want to see that smile for myself, every single day." I framed her face in my hands and gave her a light kiss before continuing. "*That* is what you bring to my life. Color. Fun. A lightness I've needed for a very long time. I want you here, with me and Owen."

She shook her head, her expression perplexed. "I don't understand. I can't just move in with you, even if I wanted to."

"Oh, yeah, right. That damn morality clause," I said, having already considered the issue. "Give me a second to rectify that situation."

Bewilderment glimmered in her eyes, but she'd understand soon enough. I left her in the living room to retrieve something from my bedroom, and when I returned, she was looking at the pop art painting, a quirky grin on her lips. She turned around to say something to me, then gasped when I opened a small black velvet box, revealing the three-carat diamond engagement ring I'd bought this week nestled inside, because I'd been prepared to fight for this woman who I knew I couldn't live without.

"Caleb…" she said, looking both shocked and startled. "What the hell?"

I chuckled. "Okay, not quite the reaction I was going for," I said, then realized I'd left out something incredibly important. "I love you, Stevie Palmer. There is nothing pretend or fake about my feelings for you. The fact that I fell in love with you so quickly and easily tells me more about who you are as a person, with so many traits that make me want to be a better man for you. I know this is unexpected, but I have every intention of marrying you, whenever you're ready. But in the meantime, as my fiancée, that means there is no longer a morality clause issue, which means you can move in with Owen and me."

Her eyes flicked from the diamond ring, up to my face, her feelings for me completely transparent, even before she spoke the words. "I love you, too, Caleb Kane," she whispered. "So much."

My heart soared. "Then marry me, so I can make you mine in every way that matters."

She nodded quickly, her face wreathed in pure joy. "Yes, I'll marry you," she said, giving me my future, my forever, with her.

EPILOGUE

Stevie

Six months later

THE OUTDOOR SPRING venue was everything I wanted it to be, despite Caleb giving me an unlimited budget for a fairytale-type wedding. Small and intimate with just forty close friends and family in attendance, the day had been perfect. Raven, Valerie, and Cara were my bridesmaids, and Owen our ring bearer.

The one thing I had splurged on was a gorgeous, custom gown in white satin and lace. One that conformed to my figure and had my new husband eyeing me possessively from across the terrace as he chatted with Remy and Dex, while I half listened to the conversation between Valerie and Jack, who'd recently moved in together. My sister was happy and secure in her new relationship, and that's all that mattered to me.

Since the day that Caleb promised to take care of the issue with Mark, there had been no more incidents. I never did ask Caleb what he'd done to make that happen, but I was grateful because it had given my sister a sense of freedom to move on with her life…with Jack.

I glanced over to the dance floor, catching sight of Cara dancing with Owen now that dinner was over and the cake had been cut. Alyssa was still in rehab and recovering, but Caleb made sure that Owen had time with his grandparents, who also occasionally took him to see his mother. Shockingly, Caleb had received a phone call from Alyssa a few weeks ago, who'd apologized for everything that had happened. Apparently, she was in counseling, and one of the things they encouraged patients to do was to try and make amends for any adverse past actions or behaviors.

Caleb, who'd been gracious and forgiving, had accepted her apology, though he'd told me after the call that he truly hoped Alyssa completed the program so she could have a better relationship with Owen.

My life seemed like a dream, and in many ways it was surreal because I never imagined that I would be one of those women who "had it all". I loved my job at Dare PR, and I now had my marketing degree. Being Owen's stepmom was a role I cherished. As of today, I was Caleb's wife and I'd never felt so adored and appreciated and loved.

And now, we had forever together, I thought, taking in the stunning bridal set on my ring finger. Which was a good thing considering just a week ago I'd discovered I was pregnant. A surprise for both of us, for sure, since having a baby now was sooner than we'd anticipated, but we were both excited to grow our family and give Owen a sibling.

"Are you ready to blow this joint, Mrs. Kane?" Caleb asked, coming up behind me and circling his arms around my waist before pressing his lips near my ear. "Because I've got at least half a dozen wicked, dirty ideas on how we'll be spending our wedding night."

I shivered, already anticipating what he had planned, and was grateful that Owen was staying with Remy and Raven for our honeymoon. "Then what are you waiting for? Let's get out of here."

His chuckle was low and sinful. "I was hoping you'd say that."

He released me, stepping around so that he was in front of me, then hoisted me over his shoulder before I realized his intent. I let out a squeak of surprise as I was tipped upside down, because it was one thing for Caleb to do the caveman routine in the privacy of our home—which he enjoyed doing to assert his dominance in a playful manner—but I couldn't believe he'd do something so blatant at our wedding.

"Everyone, have a good night," Caleb called out to our guests, drawing everyone's attention to us, much to my chagrin. "My bride and I have a marriage to consummate."

There was laughter, clapping, and cheers of encouragement as he walked out of the venue with me draped over his shoulder in my wedding gown and my cheeks burning with embarrassment.

As soon as we were enclosed in the elevator, he set me on my feet again.

"Was that *really* necessary?" I asked him, smoothing a hand down the front of my dress.

"Absolutely." He gave me one of his sexy smirks. "I just wanted to make sure you knew who's boss tonight."

"Noted," I said, always willing to concede to him in the bedroom because it was a win-win situation.

He lifted his hand and touched his fingers beneath my chin, tipping my head back so that I was staring into his now very serious eyes. His free hand very gently but protectively splayed over my still flat belly. "Are you happy?" he asked, and I knew he wasn't asking the question randomly. That my answer was important to him, especially on a day like today.

"Deliriously happy," I told him, and meant I it. "How about you?"

"More than you'll ever know," he said huskily, then dipped his head to kiss me, making me feel like nothing else mattered in that moment but the two of us, our love for each other, and the rest of our lives together.

Thanks for reading! Up next is **JUST A LITTLE DESIRE**, a story in Carly Phillips' Sterling Family world.

Other books in the Sterling Family Crossover Series:
JUST A LITTLE DESIRE

Other books in the Dare Crossover Bachelor Auction Series:
JUST A LITTLE HOOKUP
JUST A LITTLE SECRET
JUST A LITTLE PROMISE
JUST A LITTLE CHASE

For Book News:
SIGN UP for Carly's Newsletter:
carlyphillips.com/CPNewsletter
SIGN UP for Erika's Newsletter:
geni.us/ErikaWildeNewsletter

Carly Phillips and Erika Wilde Booklist

A Sterling Family Crossover Series
Just A Little Crush
Just A Little Desire

A Dare Crossover Series
Just A Little Hookup
Just A Little Secret
Just A Little Promise
Just A Little Chase

Dirty Sexy Series
Dirty Sexy Saint
Dirty Sexy Inked
Dirty Sexy Cuffed
Dirty Sexy Sinner

Book Boyfriend Series
Big Shot
Faking It
Well Built
Rock Solid

The Boyfriend Experience

About the Authors

CARLY PHILLIPS is the bestselling author of over eighty sexy contemporary romances featuring hot men, strong women, and the emotionally compelling stories her readers have come to expect and love. She is happily married to her college sweetheart and the mother of two adult daughters and their crazy dogs. She loves social media and is always around to interact with her readers. You can find out more and get two free books at www.carlyphillips.com.

ERIKA WILDE is the author of the sexy Marriage Diaries series and The Players Club series. She lives in Oregon with her husband and two daughters, and when she's not writing you can find her exploring the beautiful Pacific Northwest. For more information on her upcoming releases, please visit website at www.erikawilde.com.

Made in the USA
Middletown, DE
05 April 2025